Hannah
Mail Order Brides of Wichita Falls
CYNDI RAYE

Hannah

Mail Order Brides of Wichita Falls
Book 5

by
Cyndi Raye

---

1. http://www.CyndiRaye.com

Are you a member of my Facebook Reader's Group!
I'd love for you to join us!

Cyndi[2]Raye[3]'s Reader's Group[4]

(https://www.facebook.com/groups/

1856224058000936/?ref=bookmarks)

---

2. https://www.facebook.com/groups/

1856224058000936/?ref=bookmarks

3. https://www.facebook.com/groups/

1856224058000936/?ref=bookmarks

4. https://www.facebook.com/groups/

1856224058000936/?ref=bookmarks

Chapter 1

Max pushed at the solid, heavy front door. A pitter-patter of feet scuttled across the marble foyer then skidded to a stop. He blinked a few times before his booted heel took a step inside, noticing the gaudy furniture that stuck out like a bad mistake. A Grandfather clock ticked away in the background, the noise wearing on his tired bones.

"Welcome, Mr. Ward," the apron-wearing, petite young woman squeaked, as if afraid to speak up. She wiped her hands across the white material before clasping both hands tight in front of her.

"Relax. I'm not going to bite." Max entered the parlor. "How can anyone live in this?"

A tiny cough behind him gave him the answer he needed. No one would admit his father had been a money-grubbing evil sonofagun living in the lap of luxury who destroyed or tried to ruin those who got in his way.

"Sir, would you care for coffee, tea or something stronger?" her little voice squeaked.

Max flung his hat across the room where it landed on a settee with cushions that looked as if the upholstery was hand sewn from another century. The wood carvings on the frame stood out like a sore thumb. "Coffee, please. I have a feeling this will be a long night."

"As you wish, sir." The maid disappeared so fast Max wondered at first if he was imagining her being there. He looked back to where she had stood and shook his head. It had been a long and dreaded trip, knowing what he had to do.

Max should turn around and walk away right now. He didn't have to do this, it was a request from his aunt. More than a request, she practically got on her knees and begged him to make things right. Aunt Beth had been good to him, unlike his father, who never spared a moment of his time to pay any attention to Max, shipping him off to his aunts every chance he got.

He didn't want the tons of money from his father's estate. Max didn't need the ranch. He had a darn nice place in Arizona Territory where he lived with aunt Beth. She would never want for anything since he paid her bills. Max had worked for the railroad and invested in stocks and bonds, so he didn't have to worry too much about money. His aunt had been a famous singer at one time but all her money was gone. He had made sure his dear aunt was taken care of.

The maid returned with a shiny, fancy silver tray. A porcelain cup sat upon it. He stared.

"Sir?" Her hands began to shake. He took the tray from her, plopping it down on an Italian baroque console table with intricate designs on all four legs. The contents spilled over the edge.

The maid's eyes widened at his simple carelessness then jumped when he spoke.

"What do I call you?"

"M-Mary."

Max stirred some cream in the hot liquid and lifted the cup to his mouth. He watched Mary as she stood alone in the parlor, her hands crushed together in fear. It was his father's doing, he assumed, had always scared the daylights out of everyone in his wake. "Mary, I'm not my father. I'm here to decide what to do with all of this." A hand flew in the air, gesturing to the room. The long windows were covered by dark, heavy drapes.

"Yes, sir," she squeaked, again.

He was frustrated and disappointed. Everyone he met so far acted skittish around him. From the moment he left the train station to pick up his father's buggy in the livery, people stared and crossed the street as if he would hurt them. Taking another sip, Max put the cup down and paced the room, noticing the gaudy furniture, expensive paintings covering the walls, oriental rugs under his feet. "Will you please open these drapes?"

Mary scattered to do his bidding, pulling the expensive drapes back. Sunshine filtered through the huge windows.

"Much better. Thank you, Mary." She seemed surprised he thanked her. Max ran a hand through his hair, rubbing his jaw. It was not only going to be a huge task to get rid of all of his father's belongings but he realized this frightened woman was a reminder his father had been cruel to everyone. What had he done to her to make her so timid?

She stood at the door, waiting.

"Mary, may I ask you a question?"

She nodded, her jaw clenched together, anxiety covering her face.

"What will happen to you when I sell off these things? Will you be able to find work somewhere else?" The question was valid. He knew his father had many employees for his large estate. The ranch was huge, with a cattle ranch and working cowboys to run the whole set up. It had been basically running on its own without his father to guide things here for months.

"Perhaps the new owner will keep my grandmother and me," she whispered, her voice weak.

He nodded. "Thank you."

When she stayed glued to the floor, eyes downcast, he walked out of the room, amazed at the size of the place. He walked through the next room, a library filled with thousands of books lining a wall with a ladder to get to the top shelves.

Two other parlors were filled with more antiquated furniture, oversized paintings and objects of art. Max had no clue what to make of it all.

A bustling came up behind him as he swung around thinking someone was about to attack.

"My! My! My! If it ain't little Maximilian Ward! Come here, suga!"

Max smiled for the first time since embarking on this trip. He held out his arms wide. The old woman wrapped her arms around him and squeezed so tight he finally pulled them away. "Marni, is it really you? I thought for sure you'd be long gone by now!"

"No, child. I have nowhere else to go. Mr. Ward was an old geezer but he did pay me enough to get by on even if he scrimped on everyone else."

"It was because you took such good care of him, stood up to him, too. I remember the time I snuck out of the house to save that little duckling down by the pond. You came to my rescue and stood face to face with him so he didn't lay a hand on me."

She patted him on the cheek, then pulled on his skin like he was still seven. He covered her hand in his, surprised at the fragility of her aging fingers. "Well, perhaps I stayed because I knew you'd be back someday. Now I have another chance to take care of you. You've grown in to a fine man, Max."

Max noticed the dulling of her skin, the black hair peppered with white. She still wore it the same, pulled back in a tight bun, away from her face. The girl, who had brought him coffee now stood beside Marni. She wore her hair the same way. She even resembled Marni in a way. "Is Mary related to you, Marni?"

Marni pulled the younger girl closer. "Mary is Lizzie's daughter, my dearest and only grand daughter."

He nodded at Mary, noticing she had relaxed a bit since they first met. He spoke directly to her. "I've known your grandmother since I was born. She took good care of us all when my mother died." Max realized she had been more of a mother than his own, who disappeared from the ranch when he was two years old. He vaguely remembered how he'd cry and ask for his mother but Byron scolded and yelled at him to never mention her name again. Marni would gather him in her lap and comfort him in the kitchen where his father never stepped foot.

"She still takes care of everyone," Mary told him, her voice coming out stronger now.

"I'm sure she does. Listen, Marni. I'm here to take care of his belongings, this place. I don't know yet what to do with it all. Most likely it will be sold."

He watched how she slowly closed her eyes. Max remembered how she'd do that when he was little. When she had opened them, he often asked her what she was doing. "Praying to the good Lord above," she'd say. "Put it in his hands since mine are too full."

This job was starting to get tougher and tougher. If he thought he'd come here and dispose of everything, he forgot there were people involved. Those who depended on the wages, who needed jobs. If he took it away from these people, where would they go, what would they do? Max figured Marni was getting to old to start over. He let out a deep sigh. His observations were making it harder to just throw it all away like he had originally planned.

The man left one heck of a mess behind.

"No sense in worrying about it now, son. Let's get you settled in and something to eat. Bet you haven't eaten in hours."

Max grinned. "You know me the best, Marni. I'm starved."

"Well, then, go on. Let Mary show you to the master suite and I'll call you when supper is ready."

Max stopped at the foot of the stairs. "I'm not sleeping in the same room he did."

"I know, son. There are three other suites. Yours is on the opposite side of the house." Max nodded and followed Mary up to his suite. The room was too large for one person. A four poster bed with netting sat dead center in the middle of the room, along with more oversized furniture against each wall. A large chair with puffy cushions beckoned him.

He turned to thank Mary but she was long gone. The girl was skittish. He wondered where Lizzie, her mother was. Lizzie had been a few years older than him. He remembered playing with her when he was at the ranch, until his father sent him away to his aunt's house. As he sat back against the thick cushions, it didn't take long to find slumber.

A sharp knock woke Max. He came off the chair as if an intruder were breaking in the room. Swinging open the bedroom door, he found Mary, her hands twisted together, biting her bottom lip. "Supper is on the table, Mr. Ward."

"Call me Max, please."

"I would rather not."

"Whatever you want." After clearing his head, Max splashed water on his face from the basin on the dresser and went down to find the dining room. All he had to do was follow the delicious smell in the air. Pulling back the high back hand-tooled leather chair with garland and ribbon carvings, he sat down alone at the solid walnut dining table.

Marni brought a steaming plate piled high with fresh vegetables, mash potatoes smothered in gravy and a chunk of meat that made Max's mouth water. "I'm not eating alone," he told her. "Go get your plates and join me."

"I was hoping you'd say so," she told him, disappearing through a solid oak door. Minutes later, she was back, carting her own plate along with Mary. They sat opposite Max at the long trestle table.

As they ate together and talked some, Max realized Marni's daughter never appeared. "Where's Lizzie?"

Marni sat her fork down. Her eyes slowly roamed around the room, avoiding his gaze. "Mary, go get us some more coffee."

The young girl did as she was told. The moment she exited the room, Marni leaned in, talking softly. "She's gone, Max. Dead. No thanks to Byron. He abused her terribly. I can't speak of it in front of Mary. She witnessed the whole thing."

"He killed her?"

"May as well have. She took her own life. Walked out in the fields and let a bullet rip through her gut. Mary found her if your wondering why she is so nervous, it's the cause. She's never been the same since."

"I'm sorry, Marni." His hand reached out across the table, taking her hand to try to sooth a mother's loss.

"I planned to kill him, you know. Even if it isn't right. I know the good Lord didn't want me to entertain thoughts like that but he took her and abused her and when she told him she was in love with him, he cackled and heehawed and made fun of her, telling her she was nothing but his whore. Called her names I can't mention. Threatened her life. Instead, she took her own. Lizzie thought she was in love with him."

Max watched the old woman struggle with herself. "If it's any consolation, I would kill him if he weren't already dead for what he did to you and your family, Marni. I have to make up for this."

She shook her head, patted his hand and picked up the fork. "No sense to distraught yourself. What's done is done. I'm glad you're back, son. Even if you sell everything off, I'm glad you got a chance to come home. It's so good to see you again."

Home. This place was never home to Max. It was an ugly place where his mother disappeared one rainy night, never to be heard from again. Byron claimed she ran off, but now, Max doubted his words. It was a place he came to for brief interludes and was taken from again and again, to be pushed off to someone else. He had wanted his father's love all those years ago, up until he was a teen. Then he made the decision never to come back.

It had worked good until the old man had to go and die. It wasn't even a natural death. Texas Rangers shot him dead in the middle of a restaurant in town because he was running a rustling cattle operation and hurting people. Max also heard he was threatening a woman from town, too. The fear the old man instilled wouldn't be forgotten by the townsfolk too easily.

He would go in to town this evening to see just what Byron Ward left behind in his wake.

<> <>

Max stayed at the hotel in Wichita Falls, enjoying a hot shower along with a decent meal at Jenna's, the eatery where his father was brought to justice. Staying at the hotel overnight would give him an idea of exactly what kind of man his father had become in his last moments.

"Nice to meet a new face," Jenna told him. She was smiling until he introduced himself.

"Nice to meet you as well."

"Do you have a name, sir?" She placed a menu on the table in front of him.

"Max Ward."

Jenna stilled. "I'm sorry, what was your name again?"

"I'm not my father. Just so you know."

"I run a decent place here. You may want to not mention that name during supper hour. Most folk here have a bad taste in their mouth for Byron Ward, dead or not."

"I'm going to sell off his stuff. The ranch. Get rid of it all, wipe the man's name off the face of the earth. It's the least I can do." Max watched her closely, he didn't want to be the cause of a scene here in town. It was a nice town. He didn't remember much of it, seems there wasn't much here when he was so small. The ranch was all he had remembered.

She placed a hand on her hip. "Sell it all? What are those workers going to do? The ranch employs a lot of our townsfolk. Why, just the other day I heard from one of my patrons that since Byron was killed, the ranch was a better place to work. Why can't you let it be?"

"I never pictured myself living here, ranching on Texas land. I'll take the meatloaf."

She scribbled on her pad and placed the pencil behind her ear. Leaning forward, she said softly, "Mr. Ward, if you want to make friends here, I would suggest you turn around what your father has done. There are too many people depending on work from that ranch. It's the largest working ranch in the area. If you sell, there will be many families who will struggle."

Max drummed his fingers against the linen covered table. She was right. He was starting to see a whole new picture. If he sold off the ranch, it would most likely be bought by a big city corporation who didn't care about the families in Wichita Falls. He knew business and all these townsfolk would suffer greatly when they sent in Chinese workers who did the job for little to nothing. Same thing happened with the rail road.

Jenna brought his dinner plate, setting it down on the table. "Well, you had plenty of time to think, Mr. Ward. What's it gonna be?"

Before he could answer, a couple sat next to his table. The woman spoke up. "Ward! Oh heavens, did I hear you say this man is a Ward?"

Max looked over to see the middle aged couple staring at him like he had leprosy. The fear in their eyes was real. He wanted to reassure them but couldn't deny who he was. "I'm Max Ward."

She looked at Jenna in horror. "Is this true?"

Jenna nodded. "It's his son."

"I'm right here, listening to you both."

"Well, sir. I'm sorry to be rude but we'll take our leave and eat somewhere else." The couple got up and quickly walked to the other side of the room, taking a seat at a table in the front. He watched in dismay as they nudged the next table and poked a finger his way.

"What will they do, tell the whole darn town?" he grumbled, sticking a fork in the soft meat.

Jenna laughed. "In less than thirty minutes this whole town will know you are his son. Sometimes it is good everyone is loyal to Wichita Falls, but not so lucky for you. I'm afraid you will be shunned until you show them you are not like your father."

"How am I supposed to do that?"

"How am I supposed to know? The first thing you can do is stop trying to sell off the ranch. Show the workers you will stand by them. Then go get yourself a wife and become a decent citizen of Wichita Falls."

Max wasn't afraid of a challenge. As he ate his dinner, the thought of turning around the wrong his father imposed on this town sounded more and more like something he desired to do. It was time he showed this small town he wasn't like his father. The feeling in his gut when the couple looked at him grated on his nerves. They didn't know him and yet they were first to judge a man. It wasn't right.

"How was everything?"

"Good." He threw some coins on the table.

Jenna picked up the money, stuffing it in her pocket. "You seem like a decent man, Mr. Ward."

"Call me Max. Seems my last name is a dirty word here."

She nodded. "You can change their minds. I get the feeling you already thought about doing so."

"I suppose so. Where can I find a wife? If everyone hates my name, I won't be able to court anyone here." Max had been alone for a long time. He never had time for a lady, except when the need arose.

Jenna laughed out loud. "Go down the street to Miss Addie's boarding house. She'll match you up with a mail order bride."

"A what?"

"You heard me, a mail order bride. We have several here that found their true love. No one would know these women were mail order brides at one time."

"I'm not interested in true love, just marriage, in name only." If he were to present himself as a family man and turn the Ward name around, a bride would make him more believable. It may work after all and Marni and Mary would have a home, along with jobs for the rest of the ranch workers.

"Start with Miss Addie. She'll interview you first then send you to Daniel Ashwood, our local newspaper man, to put an ad in the papers in several cities."

He stood, determined to make things right. "Thanks, Jenna. You've been a big help."

Jenna placed a hand on her hip while balancing his empty plate in her other hand. "Just so you know, Max, I know most things that go on in this town. If you try to fool anyone, I'll be the first to know. And the first to let it be known."

"Fair enough," he replied, placing his hat on his head and headed down to Miss Addie's boarding house. Several townsfolk stared at him as he walked by. He felt their rage, heard the whispers but kept on as if he hadn't a care in the world. This was a tough lot. He had a lot to prove. He would do it, for Marni. For his aunt.

Two hours later, after an extensive interview by Miss Addie, Max got in his buggy and headed up to the newspaper office. He wanted to finish his business and get back to the ranch. Darkness was setting in the small town with a few lights here and there peeking from windows in resident's homes. The streets could use a few of those gas street lamps but he knew they were expensive. Maybe he would start off with a good deed, providing street lamps for Main Street.

When he got to the newspaper office, it was dark inside. A note on the door said *Be Back Shortly*. He stood in front of the building to wait. No sense in going home until the matter at hand was finished. Max crushed his hat between his hands, not realizing he was doing so when a man carrying a woman across the street caught his attention. The closer they got, he realized it must be the newspaper man.

"Excuse me, are you Daniel Ashwood?"

"Yes."

"I'm here to put an advertisement in the paper."

"Come back tomorrow, I'm not available right now."

"So it seems," Max answered. He watched the two who seemed to have eyes only for each other as the man held on to the woman and carried her up the steps and through the door, closing the world out behind them.

Max turned to climb back in the buggy, turning it towards the livery. He'd have to spend another night at the hotel. He snapped the reins, anxious to get the advertisement for a mail order bride started.

His life was changing like the Texas weather. He knew there was a big storm brewing.

Chapter 2

Hannah slid the money inside the wall where her step-father would never find it. She did it just in time when he stumbled through the door to her room. "Whatcha got there, girlie?"

She straightened up, sliding the picture across the hole in the wall she had made special to hide her earnings. If he found out she was skimming off the top, he'd shake her to no end. She took a few steps and put out her hand. "Here!" As some of the money she earned got swiped up in his fist, her nerves got the best of her. She worked hard every single day, longer hours than anyone else at the clothing factory. He never failed to take her money on pay day. Except she was smarter than him. She coughed, called him a drunken louse under her breath.

He counted out the money. "It's all here." Turning, he looked back, his eyes filled with greed. "Maybe you can work a few extra hours. I need more money."

Hannah stood tall, her hands clutched in her skirts where he couldn't see the fists she made. "There's no more hours at the factory. We're lucky I get ten hours a day in. Heard talk of them slowing down some this winter."

He stopped at the door. "You best hope not. I can't be living on small wages. Better look around for a second job."

Hannah stuck her tongue out as he slipped out, leaving the door open. She crossed the floor, grabbed the door and banged it shut before she turned the lock. The only way he was getting back in here was to knock it down. Although he had tried several times when he came home drunk after spending all her hard earned money, she had pushed a dresser in front of the door, laughing at his attempts to get in. He had been so drunk he probably didn't know how to turn the knob.

Most mornings she would find him face down at the kitchen table passed out, a bottle by his side. What he didn't know was she was working two more hours a day and hiding the extra money. She had told him she volunteered at the orphanage, it was her duty to do so since her mother was no longer able to. Now she wondered if her mother had done the same thing, except her mother was gone. Died of exhaustion. Hannah was not about to go down that same road, not in a city like this. Not in New York City.

She hated her step-father. Richard was mean, evil and a no-good lout who drank his life away. He had never earned a penny, expected her mother to earn the money. When she had died, he found a job at the same factory for Hannah, determined to make her his slave. Little did he know Hannah had been hiding the extra, working her fingers to the bone so she could leave and never come back. Not knowing where she would go didn't matter, only that she got away from this life.

A rapping at her bedroom window caught Hannah's attention. She ran over, slid open the lock and let her best friend inside. As the other girl climbed through the window, Hannah giggled at the sight.

"Sh, Hannah, you're going to get me in trouble."

"No, Becky, he's out cold, face in the bowl by now. Maybe I'll get lucky and he'll drown in his own dish of soup." She left him dinner warming on the stove earlier. Each night she came home, there was supper to fix before she retired to her room. Hannah didn't want to speak to her step-father although at times she had no choice.

"Here, I brought you two dollars to add to your fund."

"Are you sure? I know you need the money, too."

Becky smiled, her cheeks getting red. "I won't be needing it any longer. I'm getting married."

Hannah pushed aside the wall hanging and slid the two dollars in her hiding place. As she turned, a shadow slipped past the window. She put a finger against her mouth, quickly marching over to the window to peek out. It was quiet, too quiet, but at least there was no one there. Maybe she had imagined a shadow. She had worked so many hours with only a fifteen minute break to gobble down some bread and cheese. "All is clear.

There for a moment I thought someone was outside. Now Becky, did you tell me you are getting married? To whom? I didn't know you were even courting anyone?"

"Oh, I'm not. I found an ad for a mail order bride."

"Mail order bride! Oh, for heaven's sake! How can you trust someone you don't even know?"

Becky gave her a hug. "Hannah, does it matter? Anything has to be better than life here, working every day in that awful sewing factory, day after day after day. I want more. A husband. Children. He's a widow and has two kids, a working farm and he wants me to take care of it all."

Hannah's eyes widened. "He wants you as a slave."

Becky shook her head. "If you look at it that way. Why, I heard life is wonderful out there. Freedom to do and live as you please. I want that,

Hannah, I want it so bad I can taste it."

Hannah gave her a hug back. Who was she to be negative about her friend's dreams. "When are you leaving?"

"Tomorrow, the first train out. I haven't told a soul except for you. Here."

"What is this?" Hannah took the rolled up newspaper.

"If you have to get away, there are many ads in there, a whole column of wanted ads for mail order brides."

Hannah spewed. "I refuse to be someone's bride. When I leave, it will be on my own. I've already proven I can earn a living."

Becky turned to the window, her one leg through. "Think about it. You never know when you may need to run."

"How could you do this!" Hannah fell against the wall, her back sliding down until she sat on the floor staring in horror at the hole in the wall. The painting had been flung across the room, smashed against the dresser.

"I'll teach you to hide money from me!" Her step-father stood above her like a boar ready to pounce on its victim. His arm came out so fast it was all Hannah could do to duck. Luckily, he was too drunk to aim straight.

He leaned down, teetering a bit before his nose connected to hers. The man was getting too brave. He had never stuck his face in hers before. A tiny wisp of fear engulfed her. Hannah sucked in her breath, afraid to lash out any longer. "Girlie, hiding this from me was a big mistake. Seems like you need to be making more money now. Gonna have to hire you out to a few of my friends."

"W-what do you mean?" she stuttered, hating that she sounded so meek in front of him. She usually had the upper hand, was able to control his drunken state. He was acting so much different tonight.

He laughed, his stinky liquor breath making her gasp and hold her own. "I find myself owing a lot of money these days. I'm sure my new friends will accept you as payment."

"You can't do that." A deep fear struck her that he could do as he wanted with her. Hannah had to flee. She couldn't let this happen. But without her stash, she was stuck here in this horrid apartment with him.

"I can and I will. Next week on payday. You can bet on having a visitor or, two." He pushed himself up and staggered to the door. Turning, he laughed out loud. "I held myself back from hiring you out but after the disloyal thing you just did, I don't' give a rat's behind about you any longer."

"You never did," Hannah mumbled. She covered her face with her hands, allowing herself one cry. For fifteen minutes she shed tears, letting them stream down her face before standing up and washing them away in an act of defiance. Looking in the mirror on the wall, she stared at her red cheeks, determined to find a way out.

The rolled up newspaper caught her attention in the mirror. It still sat on her night stand as if begging her to open it up. Hannah had no choice. She wasn't about to be violated by any man. Not now, not ever. If it was going to happen, then she would be the decision maker.

Sitting on her bed, she unrolled the paper to find the advertisements. Two columns of ads stood out, but one caught her eye immediately.

Looking for a well organized lady who isn't afraid of a challenge. I own a large ranch in Wichita Falls, Texas, where I am responsible for many families, men and women. I am looking for a wife who will be at my side at all social events and help me to become a fine, upstanding citizen. This is a business only arrangement and will not expect anything more. If you are up to the challenge, please see Aloisa's Matchmaking Services on 3rd Street, who works with Miss Addie in Wichita Falls. She will interview, oversee and choose a bride. Sincerely, Maximilian Ward.

Hannah never backed down from a challenge. Rolling up the newspaper, she grabbed her coat from the rack by the front door, making her way towards 3rd street. If this was the only way to get out of this mess, then so be it. She wasn't about to become a whore for her horrible step-father.

Luckily, she was but a few blocks from the matchmaker's agency. Hannah saw the sign the moment she turned the corner. It stood out in bright yellow colors like the sun peeking out on a cloudy day. Hannah took that as a sign she was doing the right thing. She took the few steps and entered the building, a bell tinkling as she walked through the door.

A dark haired woman dressed in an elaborate two piece skirt and top with a colorful scarf around her neckline smiled and ushered her to the desk. "Sit, please. I'm Aloisa, proprietor here. I'm betting you are in desperate need of my matchmaking services?"

Hannah nodded. Was she that obvious? Scared at first, the woman put her at ease in a matter of moments. "I'm terrified my step-father has awful plans for me. Is there any available husbands immediately? I need one before next week."

Aloisa frowned. "I'm not sure I can find you one so quickly. This is almost certainly a process each time. However," she contemplated, tapping her forefinger to her chin, "there may be one here to solve your current situation."

Bustling about in her two piece dress, Hannah watched as the woman shuffled through a large pile of letters. "Aha, here it is." She put on some spectacles, pushing them down her nose and read the words to herself. "Aha, aha," she nodded while Hannah watched with trepidation. Was she really in a matchmaker's office, ready to pounce on the first offer she received?

"Maybe I'm making a mistake." Hanna rose, ready to dart out the door.

Aloisa held up her hand. "No, please, stay. This one is the perfect solution. I even have received his monies and a train ticket. Can you leave in two days?"

Hannah crushed her hands together. "Two days?" she whispered, more to herself. "I, uh, I believe I can." There really was nothing stopping her. "Can you at least tell me a bit about the man I'm going to marry?"

Aloisa folded the letter, handing it to her. "Read it on your way. Now sit back down, we need to do an extensive interview and make sure you are the right person for him, although I'm good at receiving people and I am fairly sure you are a perfect match."

<> <>

Hannah wore her Sunday best for the long ride to Wichita Falls. The colorful flowered material with orange, red and yellow hues was fading but it was all she could afford. In two days time, she had altered her mother's favorite dress to fit her. All of Hannah's work dresses were haggered and thin, not suitable at all for travel. This one, with its long sleeves and thick material would provide protection while on her long journey.

Hannah gazed at the white gloves on her hands. Even they were faded and worn. At least she had a beautiful traveling hat Aloisa had given her before she boarded the train. The woman was a saint. She had pinned the beautiful hat on Hannah's dark hair and when she saw herself in the looking glass, Hannah couldn't believe how attractive it made her feel. Blue violets adorned the dark velvet hat. It made her hair look soft and silky. At least she would appear to her intended looking like a well-maintained lady, even if she was not. Long days at the factory gave little time to dote on her appearance. Most nights she was to tired to do anything more than to make supper and fall in to bed.

Those days were over. Hannah was free of her stepfather's rule and she would never, ever go back. Even if this mail order bride situation didn't work out, she would find a way to survive without having to go back to that evil man.

A whistle blew in the distance. The conductor announced two minutes until Wichita Falls. Excitement coursed through her veins. This is it, she told herself. *Don't be afraid, you can do this!* Her hands squeezed around the handle of her small carpetbag. She didn't have much to bring along, a nightgown and two other dresses. The rest she left behind, even though she only owned four dresses.

Her new husband would have to understand. She stretched her neck to see if he was already on the platform at the train station, but it was too hard to see that far ahead. Hannah's heart began to pump so fast, she placed a hand over it to still the beating, thinking those around her could hear.

A few minutes later she found herself standing on the platform, waiting as men and women walked by her. Several men walked towards her but then turned to meet up with someone else. Hannah began to worry. She bit her bottom lip, tapping her fingers on the carpet bag handle. Where was her husband to be? Had he forgotten?

The conductor yelled out over the platform the train would be leaving in two minutes. "All aboard!" he said for the last time before disappearing.

Hannah was alone when the train shook the platform as it left the small prairie town. She looked ahead to see houses and small business's on either side of a dirt street. Sooner or later she would have to walk down that street to find her husband to be, who obviously was late. Or, perhaps, not coming at all. Had he changed his mind? Luckily, there was some money left over from travelling. She doubted it would be enough to live on for more than a week or so.

Hannah was not the type to panic. Not yet. She was strong and brave and held her chin up as she made her way down the steps from the train depot. Squaring her shoulders, she stood for a few more minutes and waited. She'd give Mr. Ward one more chance to show up.

The fear seared inside of her but she wasn't going to show it outwardly. If there was one thing losing her mother proved, it was Hannah could persevere in the worst conditions. Being stranded in a prairie town, thousands of miles from home was nothing compared to the awful horror her step-father had in store for her.

No. She was better off here even if this man never showed. She would make her own way. Some way. Somehow. A new opportunity was right in front of her.

Beads of sweat began to form under the brim of her hat. Hannah took her gloved hand to wipe her brow. How long had she stood here? Her head jerked around to a side street where a dark brown buggy with a beautiful horse trotted towards the train station. The buggy stopped, forming a cloud of dust in front of her.

She could barely see the man holding the reins. He jumped from the buggy and stood before her. Taking her carpetbag, he looked down at her and smiled.

Goodness gracious, the man had the most charming smile she had ever seen. He tipped his hat back, removed it, revealing dark, thick hair and nodded. "My deepest apologies. I find myself running late most days. There's so much to do." His deep voice was strong and solid. She liked the way he spoke, looking directly at her as if he was interested in what she had to say.

It didn't take much for Hannah to forgive his tardiness. She smiled. "You must be Mr. Ward."

"I am, although you may want to call me Max. Seems my name is not too popular in the public eye."

Hannah tilted her head. "Oh?" What kind of man didn't want to speak his last name? Was he a wanted man? An outlaw?

She took a step back. "I'm afraid you will have to explain this to me, sir. I'm not inclined to go off with a man with a bad reputation."

He held out his arm. "Please, don't fear. It was my father's doing. I'll explain it all on our way to the church."

"Church?"

He nodded, raising his brow. "You did read my letter, did you not? I explained clearly I needed a bride immediately. It was why I sent the money along with the advertisement."

That would explain why she had no more than two days to pack and leave, except Hannah didn't realize it would happen so fast. "Well, then, sir. Let's go to the church," she told him, sounding a lot braver than she felt.

He helped her in the buggy and secured her carpetbag on the floor. Taking the reins, Hannah noticed how tanned and muscular those hands and forearms were. He obviously was a man who worked the land. She could tell right away he wasn't a lazy man like her step-father.

"I'll have to confess I didn't read your letter. I stuffed the envelope in one of my skirt pockets and then left the dress behind.

I meant to read it on the train ride here but of course realized too late it was back in New York."

He gazed over at her, a grin on his face. "I honestly can't remember what all I wrote in those letters. Ah, here's the church." He got out of the buggy and helped her down, taking her arm gently as he guided her to the church. A door flew open.

"About time. We don't have all day," a large man told Max. "I'm not sure I should even be performing this marriage but if you keep your word that you will fix your daddy's wrongs, then so be it. A man's gotta have a second chance."

Hannah, confused as ever, followed Max inside. They stood at the alter, where a woman who introduced herself as the preacher's wife, waited with a small bouquet of flowers.

Hannah held on to Max's arm a bit tighter than she realized. He patted her arm with his free hand, leaning over. "It will be alright. You'll get used to the rough people here."

Hannah wondered if she would.

"Welp," the preached began. "I'm Reverend Daniel Conners, this here is my wife, Mrs. Conners. We need two witnesses but since no townsfolk wanted to do so, I found the only one willing to stand in. Get on over here!"

An old man, who was slouched on one of the benches rose and swaggered his way to the alter. Hannah looked in shock as the man staggered towards them, leaning on a bench so he didn't fall over. He hadn't even dressed for a wedding. Wearing a pair of pants with suspenders and a button down shirt that seen better days, he reeked of alcohol. Hannah placed her gloved finger over her nose.

"Sorry, ma'am," the preacher apologized. "Town drunks the only witness I could find. Let's get on with it."

Hannah and Max looked at each other and sighed.

Chapter 3

"You may kiss the bride."

Hannah hadn't been paying attention to any of Reverend Conners words. She knew this was a farce, a business agreement and so she had tuned him out. Until he said those last words.

Max's hands felt warm on her shoulders as he leaned down and placed a kiss on her mouth. She lifted her chin to meet his, thinking she would receive a small, friendly peck. After all, this was business only.

That didn't happen. The moment their mouth's touched and his warm breath mingled with hers, she drew him in like a butterfly encasing the freedom of leaving the cocoon. It couldn't be helped. Hannah had never experienced a kiss quite like this before.

To be honest, no one had ever kissed her. She had been a slave to her step-father for so many years, the thought of dating never crossed her mind.

That's why she was knocked for a loop when they kissed. Her gloved hands wrapped around his neck, her fingertips digging into his skin. When he moaned in her mouth it encouraged her more. A power so strong engulfed her, Hannah realized with just a kiss she could control a man. She liked that. Taking a step closer, she pushed her lips in to his, teasing, enticing him, until she felt his hand on her chin before sliding down her neck towards her collar.

Someone cleared their throat.

Max stepped away.

Hannah wanted to be ashamed but she wasn't. She liked the kiss. Her first kiss. Her gloved hand went to her lips. They felt bruised, in a good way. She smiled. The preacher's wife, her eyes downcast, pressed her mouth together in the background as if she were trying not to smile.

Max stared at her mouth so hard as if he wanted to get back to kissing. Then he turned to the preacher. "Sign the document. We must get back to the ranch."

He was all business now but Hannah tasted him moments before. Under her kisses, he seemed so out of control. She knew this new found power was going to be interesting to say the least.

Max took her hand and placed it on his arm as they left the church. He was silent as he helped her in to the buggy. That's when her stomach let out a growl.

Embarrassed, she giggled.

He grinned. "We should get you something to eat before we leave."

"I'm sorry. I was too nervous to eat on the last leg of the train ride."

"That settles things." He helped her back out of the buggy and guided her towards the small eatery beside the hotel.

Jenna's Place was the only fine-dining restaurant in Wichita Falls. It was quaint and had a woman's touch with round tables covered in pretty white tablecloths. A single candle flickered in the center of each table.

The late afternoon crowd was beginning to arrive for supper. As the newly wedded couple waited for someone to seat them, several others pushed past Max and Hannah, drawing the attention of the young serving girl.

A couple who pushed their way ahead of them called out to the young girl. "Sallie Mae, we'll take the seat by the window over there, away from the riff-raff."

Sallie Mae waved them on, glaring at Max when she noticed him standing there. Hannah took it all in, watching the cords on his neck tighten when she deliberately turned away. For some reason, he was being ignored.

Hannah spoke up. "We don't have to dine here. I'm fine until we get back to your ranch."

Max turned to her. "We'll wait."

The look on his face told her he wasn't going to budge on his decision. There was more going on here than Hannah realized but in order to figure it all out, she needed food. "Pardon me," she told him. "I'll be right back."

Hannah marched up to the young serving girl. "Sallie Mae?"

She turned to Hannah with a smile. "Yes, ma'am?"

"I would like to sit at the small table in the corner if that is alright with you."

"Certainly. Help yourself. I'll be with you shortly."

"Fine. When you make it to our table, please bring along a bottle of wine."

"Yes, ma'am."

She walked back to where Max was standing, took his hand and led him to the corner table. Smiling, she waited for him to pull out a chair.

Max took off his hat and sat down across from Hannah. The candle flickered and left shadows on the white linen tablecloth. He grinned. "This is the first time I got a table in under twenty minutes."

She placed her hands over his. "Max, what in the world is going on here? It was obvious Sallie Mae was not going to seat you."

He shrugged. "Sooner or later she'd have to seat me. Especially since Jenna, the owner, would eventually come out of the kitchen to see how everyone is doing."

"That's awful!" Hannah was not going to like it here if everyone was horrible to each other. "Does this happen often?"

"Every time I come to Wichita Falls, which is once or twice a week. I've tried to be friendly but a man can only take so much rejection."

He didn't seem too upset that others treated him badly.

"I need to know what happened here, Max."

He leaned back in his chair and sighed. "My father, that's what happened. He was evil, paid lousy wages and worked his employees to the bone. He hurt people, badly. There was a woman here he was determined to have as his own. Almost destroyed her but she fought back. He rustled cattle which caused his demise."

"I think I'm seeing the picture. Where were you when all of this took place?" She doubted he was in the picture until recently.

"At my ranch in Arizona."

"That explains things. Well, Max, we have a lot of work to do if what you are looking for is to restore your family name." It was as if she could read what was going on in his head. Or, perhaps, he wanted the same things she did, a place to feel welcomed, a family and town to belong in.

"I have a lot of people depending on me. If it weren't for that, I'd sell everything and go back to my aunt's ranch. But I have to turn this around before I can go anywhere. It's why I ordered a mail-order bride."

"I've never backed down from a challenge."

Max grinned. "Me neither. I think I'm going to like being married to you, Hannah."

She watched his mouth, knowing he was staring at her. When she looked in to his beautiful, dark eyes, she knew he was thinking the same thing she was, about that kiss they had shared earlier.

<><>

Max watched her eyes widen at the sight of the ranch house.

"It's huge!" he heard her gasp.

"Welcome to Ward Ranch."

"We are to live here?"

"Yes. Of course. Where else would we live?" Max stopped the buggy out front and threw the reins to a ranch hand waiting to take the horse back to the stables. Max took her arm and guided her to the front of the house.

"The porch is bigger than my whole apartment in New York City," she told him.

"Wait until you see the way my father lived. It's too much for even me and I'm used to nice things."

"Well, what are we waiting for?" Hannah pushed open the front door to be greeted by a smiling older woman with gray hair and wrinkled cheeks. A young girl, maybe twelve at the most, stood beside her, half hidden behind her skirts.

"I'd like you to meet Mrs. Hannah Ward, my wife." Max said the words with pride. He was certain Marni was overjoyed he brought a wife home. Why, having another woman in the house will be the highlight of her day. He knew Hannah was about to be spoiled silly.

"Miss Hannah, welcome to the Ward Ranch. I'm Marni and this is my grand daughter Mary. Pleased to meet you." Then the old woman opened her arms and gave Hannah a great big old fashioned hug. She smacked her lips on Hannah's cheek and pinched her cheeks while hooting and hawing about how pretty she was.

Max grinned at Hannah when she looked at him in surprise. He shrugged. It was Marni's personality, she was such a loving lady and if she gave Hannah a hug like that, it meant she was accepted by the old woman.

"It is a pleasure to meet you, Marni, and Mary." Hannah leaned down a bit and took Mary's hand in hers, trying to make the girl feel like a part of this. Max noticed how Mary shied away, pulling her hand back.

He watched Hannah's reaction. A puzzled look shaded her eyes for a mere second and then she pulled her shoulders back and gave Mary the biggest smile ever. Max's heart swelled. Marni and Mary were two of the few people he loved. Saddened by the fact he left here and never came back to check on them, he was determined now to take care of them both, no matter what. Even if he had to stay here and make a life at this ranch, he would.

He could always sell the ranch in Arizona and move his aunt here. She had wanted to come along but he wasn't sure what he would find. He couldn't bring her here, yet. Not until the town accepted him first.

A heavy sigh left his chest. The burden of undoing what his father had done lay heavy on his soul. It ate away at Max day and night. He could barely stand being in the house with all the gaudy, over priced furniture.

"Max?"

Hannah's gentle touch stirred him from those terrible thoughts. He turned to her to find her staring at his hands, which were crushing his hat into a ball. He let go, not realizing what he had been doing.

"I'm taking your wife to the kitchen for some refreshments and to show her around. You, young man, have some messages to attend to. Mr. Youngston was here earlier. I left them on your desk." Marni shuffled Hannah through the door to the kitchen, talking away and moving her hands back and forth like she was putting out a fire.

"Yes, Marni." He turned away from the ladies and worked his way to his study, where he found a pile of paperwork dead in the center of the large intricately carved wooden desk. Max took off his jacket, opened the two top buttons of his shirt and rolled up his sleeves. This was going to be a long night of reading documents signed by his father. The deals he made with others were all crooked and the offers were meant to benefit Ward Ranch and not the recipient.

Max read a few, disgusted, then tossed them on the desk. He leaned back in the padded chair, closing his eyes. Bryon Ward had been a jerk. The way he had manipulated every single person he made a deal with was too overwhelming. Max's brain hurt thinking about how to make it all right with every single person who had dealings with him. Several townsfolk were about to lose their homes because the interest rate his father charged was outrageous. No working man could keep up with those payments.

"A penny for your thoughts?" Her gentle voice softly caressed his overburdened ears. He sucked in a deep breath, turning towards the angelic voice. She stood at the door, a cup in her hand, looking nervous.

"Come in, take a seat."

Hannah set the cup down in front of him. She took a step back.

"Please, sit for awhile," he offered, his hand pointing towards the chair opposite the desk. She did.

"This house is quite the show place," she told him in a soft voice as though she didn't want to disturb the quiet in the room.

"This house is ridiculous. It's filled with items no one would ever use or need. I've a mind to sell the whole lot."

"I'm afraid I'm in agreement with you, Max." Her soft spoken voice when she said his name made his gut tighten. He was starting to like Hannah. She was so beautiful with dark, almost black, silky hair and flawless skin, a perky nose and those eyes, they looked at him as if he were the only person in the world she wanted to talk to. When they were at Jenna's earlier, she had paid attention to his words as if he were the only patron in the restaurant. As if he were the only man she ever had an interest in.

He had to get rid of these thoughts. This was a business arrangement, made by him. He couldn't change the rules now. Not until he made a place in this town where people didn't hate the name Ward. "I'm glad I'm not the only one who thinks my father had terrible taste in furniture."

"Those drapes look like they belong in a museum in New York City."

Max grinned.

Hannah smiled.

Max's gut tightened again.

"And those gaudy statues of women on the table against the wall," she mentioned, laughter in her voice.

"Have you seen the ones in your bedroom suite?" His brow rose, knowing she was in for a surprise when she went upstairs. His father had bad taste in art, even though he would never judge a piece of art, but this whole place, filled with so much, was too much for one man.

"I'm afraid I may faint if it is anything like these," she joked.

"Perhaps I should escort you to your suite then, to catch you if you fall." Why did he say that? Her sudden ghastly look told him he went too far. Or, was it fear? He leaned closer. Yes, it was fear. He had to reassure her he would not overstep his boundaries. "A mere joke, Hannah. Please, I like when you smile."

She did then, relief showing in those dark eyes.

There was something deep in her eyes that told of secrets held there. What was she afraid of, a man's touch? By rights, they were married, he could attend to her in the bedroom if he so wished. But he had made a contract with his bride, a business arrangement and he was not one to go against his word. "My word is my honor," he told her, his own dark eyes staring in to hers.

"I trust you." Those three words knocked him for a loop. She was one of two people in the surrounding area who did. Everyone else thought he was going to be like his father. "Sadly, you and Marni are the only two people right now who do."

She reached across the desk, taking his hand. The softness of her fingers against his made him so aware of her. "Then it's time we begin to change that, Mr. Ward. I'm happy to help and I think I may know how."

"How?"

"Well, as I sit here realizing we both hate all this furniture and art, why not replace it with what we like?"

"We could do that, yes." He still didn't get what she was trying to say.

"We need to go back to the town of Wichita Falls and find out what they need the most. A school? A library, museum? I see they have a church so that's out. What is it the town needs the most? When we find out, we'll have an auction, sell all this stuff and buy the town that very thing."

He grinned. "You, Mrs. Ward, are brilliant. We'll go first thing in the morning. Care to take a stroll outside before we retire?" He stood and held out his arm.

As she placed her fingers over his muscled forearm, he felt the tightening again. Was Max going to be able to keep his hands to himself?

"We'll make great business partners, Max." Her words were like a splash of cold water in his face.

He opened the front door for her. "Great ones," he told her, wondering what he had gotten himself in to.

Chapter 4

"He left you a note," Marni told her when she sat at the breakfast table. Hannah had taken a stroll around the property with Max last night, a half moon and clear sky with thousands of sparkling stars lighting their path. It was romantic to say the least, but they weren't having a romantic moment. They were business partners and Max had made that clear. Except he kept touching her hand whenever he spoke to her and once he pushed a strand of fly-a-way hair from her cheek, letting his fingers linger there for a brief second.

"Thank you." She took the note and opened it. *Hannah, I'm sorry I can't take you in to Wichita Falls this morning. There is a problem on the ranch I have to attend to. Once it is taken care of, we can arrange to do this another day. Your business partner (grin), Max, P.S. I had a nice time on our stroll. It was so relaxing I fell right to sleep. Haven't done that since I got here.*

Thank you.

Please turn around.

She turned to find a vase filled with daisies on the table by the small window that looked out over one of the gardens. Hannah rose out of her chair. "What did he do, buy these for me?" No one ever bought her anything, not since her mama died. That seemed like ages ago.

Marni stood beside her. "He picked them for you. I saw him barefoot out in the garden early this morning. Don't tell him I said so."

A swell of pride at the image of Max out in the gardens picking her flowers filled her head. "That is so darling."

"He won't feel so darling when Georgie finds out someone was trampling about in his flower gardens. But I ain't gonna squeal on my boss." Marni laughed, her eyes filled with the love she had for Max.

Hannah was beginning to feel so much affection for this woman. "You care about him very much, don't you, Marni?"

"Let's sit and have some breakfast and I'll tell you all about him, from the time he was a little lad up until he left here for good.

<> <>

Hannah had decided Max had way too much going on at the ranch so she asked Marni if there was anyone else who could take her to Wichita Falls. Georgie, the gardener, knew how to drive a buck board and said he needed to go get some more flower seeds and could do it right after lunch.

The ride was bumpy. She sat alongside Georgie on the wooden bench, who didn't speak much. He was much older than anyone she had ever known, with fine wrinkles dotting his entire face. His skin was tanned from spending endless hours in the gardens. The older man was tense and quiet, so she left him alone.

She let her thoughts drift to Max. He was so adamant about clearing his last name and she didn't blame him one bit. As his wife, it was her duty to help, because that's what this business arrangement was all about. Hannah never did anything half-way. She'd give her all and help him clear the Ward name. Perhaps things weren't all that bad and Max just needed to be nicer to the townsfolk.

The first stop she made was to the mercantile. Several folks were in the store. After she entered, the room fell silent where a few seconds ago she had heard talking and laughing. Was this what Max heard whenever he walked into a public area?

Riff-raff was mumbled by an older patron who grabbed her sack off the counter and marched out the door. The tinkling of bells above seemed so loud in the quiet store.

Hannah placed her chin in the air, turned to the man behind the counter and smiled, although it was a forced one. She would not let them bring her down. If she could face her step-father each day then this would be a breeze. "I would like to purchase some material."

"I'm out of here, have a good one, Jim," another patron mumbled. He steered clear of Hannah and stared as if she were a boil on his nose.

Hannah opened her mouth to tell him what she thought and then clamped down. Angry words would get her nowhere. She turned back to the store owner. "Jim, is it?"

"It's Mr. Wheeler to you," he said, his voice gruff. "Make it quick, I'm off to pick up some supplies at the train depot."

Hannah knew it was a lie. She had an itinerary in her reticule of when the train ran for the next few weeks. She had picked one up when she got here, in case things hadn't worked out with Max and she had to leave here in a hurry. She wasn't a fool. She didn't know what to expect when she got here to Wichita Falls and Hannah always tried to be prepared.

She got to thinking it was better to be sweet and nice than to tell him she knew he lied. "I would like a few yards of material there," she pointed.

The mercantile owner cut the material and rolled it, tied a string around the middle and took his good old time. Hannah found herself tapping her toe on the floor waiting. His claim of being in a hurry was another attempt to scare her off.

When he finished and told her the price, she gasped. "That's robbery!"

"It's my store. I can charge whatever I want to." A smirk crossed the man's face. He was being obnoxious and didn't try to hide it.

Digging in her reticule, she counted out her money. "Mr. Wheeler, I don't have enough, it seems." She hadn't thought it would cost so much for some material to make curtains. This was deliberate because of who she was married to.

"Well, then, guess you can't buy the material, Mrs. Ward." He spat out the last name like it was poison on his tongue.

"Do you have a tab in Mr. Wards name I can place it on?"

The older man laughed out loud but it wasn't pleasant at all. "A tab! Not on your life, missy! Now, go on, take yourself out of my store."

"But, but I need decent curtains," she protested.

"Go on now, closing up. You take yourself right out of here before I have to get mean."

Offended, Hannah stared at the man, shocked at his behavior. She pulled her shoulders back, pursed her lips and turned her back on him. "It would serve you right if you had some competition here. Maybe another mercantile to bring your prices down."

He grunted. "No one would buy anything from a Ward owned store."

Hannah had never been treated so badly. She came out of the mercantile with empty hands. Her sole purpose was to buy some material to replace those heavy, awful curtains in the house.

The next two stops were a repeat of the mercantile. Hannah was determined not to let the townsfolk's attitude get the best of her. She stopped in at Jenna's for some tea but found the same young girl serving again. The one that treated Max so badly during their dinner last night. Hannah waited over ten minutes to be seated. Finally, she marched to the first available table and sat down, daring the young server to say a word. Eyes flashing, she set her reticule on the table, her back straight and watched the girl. Another twenty minutes went by while the girl served other customers, who avoided Hannah as well. No customer in the restaurant would acknowledge her.

The term riff-raff was starting to grate on her nerves. Whispering it as they passed by Hannah's table forced her to keep her head down, quietly reading the menu that she had almost memorized. She would not shed a tear, not over a bunch of small-minded people.

"Well, hello, may I help you?"

Relief went through her as she looked up to see the beautiful Jenna at her table. "Thank you," was all she could muster.

Jenna stared at a few of her customers before pulling the chair across from Hannah and sitting down. "Do you mind?" she asked Hannah.

"Not at all. It must be very lonely for Max. These people are terrible."

"I agree."

The moment Jenna sat down the young girl was at the table.

"Sallie Mae," Hannah acknowledged. "May I please have a cup of coffee?"

"Yes, ma'am," she said, her voice sweet, her button nose no longer up in the air.

"Jenna, would you care for anything?"

"Yes, bring me a cup and a plate of pastries. My new friend and I have lots to talk about."

Before Hannah realized what happened two cups of coffee with all the makings and a plate of delicious looking pastries were placed on the linen tablecloth.

Jenna placed her elbows on the table. "It seems I heard rumors that Jim Wheeler wanted to overcharge for some material, is that right?"

She nodded. "How did you find out so fast?"

Jenna laughed out loud. "Within five minutes of you walking in to that store, the whole town knew you were there. Word travels fast here. If I may suggest something, I would propose you stop by the newspaper and ask for a copy of the weekly news. Go through the advertisements until you find the one to order you a Sears Catalog. You can buy whatever you want and have it shipped on the rail road. Jim Wheeler has one but I doubt he'll let you use his."

"Thank you. I doubt I'll ever go back in that store again. It's like being in the middle of a robbery what he charges!" Jenna laughed, her sweet smile helping Hannah to relax. "I didn't think it would be so difficult. I left the mercantile and stopped by the little shop to buy some tea for Marni, our cook. But the Chinese lady pretended she didn't speak English and refused to wait on me."

"I know, I heard that, too."

Hannah shook her head. "You obviously hear it all, don't you, Jenna?"

Jenna nodded. "Everyone eats here sometime or other. I can hear everything going on when I'm in the back cooking. I'm sorry you and your husband are being treated poorly. Don't give up, people have a tendency to forgive and forget sooner or later."

"I have to do something to help him."

Jenna drew a pastry from the plate and took a small bite. Placing the napkin over her mouth, she dabbed it along the corners.

"I'm afraid that may take some time, but don't fret, when they see you are not here to hurt them, they will change their minds."

"Max and I both plan to turn things around. He was saying how he hated all the glitz and glamour his father acquired. Awful furniture and paintings cover his house from floor to ceiling. I suggested to Max we should sell every single piece of furniture and start over."

Jenna set her cup down. "That's a great idea. It may turn some people here to another way of thinking."

Hannah bit her bottom lip. "As I was walking today I didn't see a school. Does Wichita Falls have a school?"

"No. Are you thinking what I'm thinking?" Jenna took Hannah's hand and squeezed.

"Yes. We'll have a big auction and all the proceeds can go to building a school, even if we have to add some of the Ward money afterwards."

"We're going to need a school teacher."

"Oh, I didn't think that far ahead."

"No worries. We can advertise for one. I'm sure there will be many applicants. What teacher wouldn't want a brand new school to run?"

"Perfect." Hannah stood up. "I'll run this all by Max this evening."

Jenna stood and gave Hannah a hug. "Keep me informed. I'll do all I can to help."

"You are a nice friend, Jenna. Thank you for welcoming me to Wichita Falls. Unlike some others here." She had to say it, she was tired of people staring at her back.

Jenna whispered in her ear. "You tell 'em, Hannah. Don't put up with their nonsense."

Hannah was smiling as she made her way to the buck board. Georgie was waiting patiently, his eyes closed, arms crossed as if napping. When he she appeared, his eyes opened. He started getting down from the buck board so he could help her up.

A horse and rider came flying out of nowhere while Hannah was crossing. It didn't slow down but swerved around her, causing her to stumble. Startled, she tumbled head first on to the dirty street, her face crashing against the ground. She had tried to put out her hands for protection but failed. Her right arm hit the ground as a searing pain shot clean through, all the way up to her shoulder. Hannah cried out.

"Mrs. Ward!" Georgie yelled, scrambling faster than a man his age should. He bent down in the middle of the street to help her up, crooning like a mother hen. "Come now, misses. Let's get you in the wagon."

Hannah felt as if a herd of cattle trampled over top of her. With shaky knees, Georgie helped her across the rest of the street. He made her sit in the back of the wagon where she could stretch out her legs and lean against the side. Then he placed a small lap blanket over her knees. "Now you sit right there. I'm getting you back to the ranch."

Georgie was careful to take off slowly. Hannah was glad. Each bump took a toll on her body, the pain from falling shooting through every inch. As she glanced out across the street, men and women both mingled on front porches, watching. Not one person offered any help. The horse and rider had stopped at the saloon, slid off his horse and stumbled through the front door. She took it all in like a free play she had the chance to watch in New York City's park a long time ago.

Hannah wanted to raise her fist and shake it at the townsfolk. Refraining from doing so, she raised her good arm to swipe loose hair from her brow. Her hair had fallen out of the pins, which were lying in the street somewhere. Dark hair, almost black, tumbled down her back, flowing over the back of the buck board in silky waves. She leaned her head back, closing tired eyes. How in the world would she turn things around when all the town wanted to do was punish them for the sins of the father? It was going to be a struggle and a fight to win these townsfolk over. They were a tough lot.

Max nudged the stallion forward. Finishing earlier than expected, he came back to take Hannah to town but found out she had already headed there with Georgie. Little did she know the townsfolk were not going to be receptive. They would treat her as bad if not worse than they treated him, knowing she was the wife of the dreaded Mr. Ward.

Max knew she didn't realize how people were here. He didn't blame her for wanting to go to town but he had to warn her, make sure she was ok. His brow formed beads of sweat as he worked the horse faster to get to Wichita Falls.

When he saw the buck board in the distance, relief washed over him. That was a short trip, he thought, then squinted his eyes when he noticed Georgie was alone. *Where was Hannah?*

"Come on, git," he ordered the horse, digging his heels in a little harder. She immediately obeyed, rushing towards the wagon like her tail was on fire.

When Georgie saw the rider, he slowed down and waved. "Mr. Ward! Mr. Ward!"

That's when Max spotted the long mane of waves flowing like a river from the wagon. A gut-wrenching fear caught him off-guard. He pulled on the reins, jumping off the horse before it stopped completely and ran towards her. "Hannah!"

She turned towards his voice, her eyes fluttering open. Max jumped in the back of the wagon, falling to his knees. He took her face in his hands. "What happened?"

Georgie ranted on, spilling words out so fast it was hard to keep up. "Some careless rider came barrelling down the street while she was crossing. She began crossing the street and I no more 'n jumped down to help Mrs. Ward when the rider practically knocked her over."

"Who was the rider?"

"Don't know, sir. The man went in to the saloon. Never stopped or made any apologies."

Max fumed. The whole side of her face was bruised and turning purple from the fall. She held her forearm with one hand and winced when he began to push on her shoulder to see if there was any broken bones. "Hannah, I'm going to get you to a doctor. Georgie, take my horse and go get the doc. Tell him I'll pay him triple to come out right now." The older man did as he was told, hesitating at first before he climbed on the stallion. After several minutes, Georgie got control of the big boy and took off in to town like a man on a mission.

Max took his place on the wooden seat, making sure Hannah was as comfortable as possible. "I'll get you back to the house, darling. Hang on."

His insides were doing flips as they made their way to the main house. Max hadn't realized what seeing her hurt would feel like. He thought he no longer had any emotions left. He was wrong.

Within such a short timing of knowing her, he wanted to protect this woman who traveled all this way to find a new life.

Emotions tugged at Max like nobody's business. He would find out who hurt her and make them pay one way or another.

Chapter 5

Marni came running from the house the moment the buck board came to a halt, her hand favoring her hip. "What happened?"

Max lifted Hannah up. "She's hurt. Someone tried to run her over."

Hannah moaned softly when he took her in his arms and began to carry her inside. Max brushed his lips across her hair, pressing softly. "Everything is fine now, Hannah. Your home."

Marni followed behind, ordering Mary to get some water boiling. He carried her to her suite and placed her body gently on her bed after Marni rolled down the cover. Max sat on the edge of the bed holding her hand.

"I'm fine," she whispered, exhaustion evident in her voice.

Max brought her hand to his mouth. He held her sweet skin there for a moment until Mary came through the door with a bowl of warm water and some clean rags. Dipping one cloth in the water, Marni blotted it on her cheeks. She winced.

"Let me do that," Max ordered. "Marni, can you go wait for the doctor. He should be coming along shortly."

Mary stood by Max watching as he carefully squeezed the cloth again, cleaning her face, erasing the dust from the street.

"That feels nice," Hannah whispered, her voice barely audible. She blinked several times. "I'm sorry, Max."

The cloth stilled against her cheek. "What are you sorry for, Hannah? It isn't your fault someone else was so careless."

"People are mean. I wanted to buy material for curtains. That old coot in the mercantile tried to charge me triple the cost."

Max tried to control his temper. "Hannah, did someone mistreat you?"

"They don't like me. Or you." Her eyes flew open. He watched her struggle with trying to stay awake.

Max turned to Mary. "Go see if the doctor is on his way. Hurry."

"I'm fine, Max. Let me sleep and I'll be fine."

From experience, Max knew she didn't dare fall asleep. He felt around her head, pressing gently along her hairline to make sure she didn't have any lumps from the fall. Sure enough, a small knot on the side near her temple stuck out like a sore thumb. He placed the warm cloth over the lump, making her wince. "I'm afraid you can't go to sleep yet. You may have a concussion."

She yawned. Max took another pillow and pulled her forward, placing it behind her head. He was concerned about her arm. She was still holding it with her other hand. Someone would pay for this, he vowed. Getting the townsfolk to accept him was one thing but he would not tolerate abuse.

Doc Smith was really an animal doctor, not so much for humans but he was all the town had. Max wasn't too pleased about that and vowed to hire a doctor himself after this was all over. This town would change their ways and he'd be the one to make sure they did, even if he had to spend every dime of his fathers to do so.

The doc came in through the door protesting how he had to birth some calves over on the Zimmers farm and this would tie him up.

"I'm paying triple what they pay you, Doc. I need you to check my wife." There was no arguing with Max. He stood up, nose to nose with the tall doctor, daring him to refuse.

"I guess I can take a look."

"Someone tried to run her over." Max's flat statement had the doctor raising a brow.

"I can hardly believe that. Who says?"

"Georgie, my gardener. He saw the whole thing." Most people in the area knew Georgie to be an upright citizen of Wichita Falls.

"I'm sorry, son. That's no way to treat a young lady." The doc pressed around her shoulder for some time, determining there were no broken bones. He moved away from Hannah and motioned for Max to come outside. "Miss, you make sure she doesn't fall asleep," he ordered Mary before they went out the door..

"Yes, sir." Mary took Hannah's hands and began to ask her questions to keep her awake.

When the two were alone in the hallway, the doc turned to Max.

"She's got quite the goose egg on her head. Close to the temple. You're going to have to keep her awake for at least a few more hours to make sure she doesn't fall in to what they call a coma."

"I suspected as much," Max told him. "What about the arm? She was favoring it on the way back."

"We'll make a sling for her to keep it tight against her body so she can't move it. I suspect it's a sprain. Keep the fluids moving. Don't leave her alone for the next day or so."

"Thanks, doc." Max pulled money from his pocket and stuffed it in the doctor's hand. "Come back and check on her in a few days."

He looked down at the amount of money in his hand and nodded. "I will. Now let's get back in there and finish up. I have a calf to birth." His gruff demeanor took some getting used to but he had taken care of Hannah and that's all Max cared about.

The doc placed a sling around Hannah, securing the arm so it would not move much. Hannah seemed more awake now, her eyes tired but yet more focused. "Young lady, I'm afraid you'll have to stay awake for a few more hours. Mr. Ward will make sure of it. I'll be back in a few days and we'll see about removing the sling."

Doc left, nodding to Max as he hurried away. Max helped Hannah out of bed, wrapping his arm around her as they made their way to the balcony doors. "I think we'll get some fresh air, darling."

Hannah smiled at him but didn't speak at first. She sighed. Her body pressed against his side as if comfortable leaning in to him. Max held her even closer while they stood for some time watching the landscape, miles and miles of Texas Prairie that met the azure blue sky. The sun was beginning to fade some, drawing the clouds closer to mother earth. "It's beautiful here."

Max leaned in and kissed her hair. "I hadn't bothered to look until now. Been focused on my father's mess. You're right."

"I'm beginning to think the rider deliberately tried to run me over."

"I suspected as much. Don't you worry, Hannah, I'll get to the bottom of this."

"I'm worried, Max. Do you think they would actually harm us to get us to move away? I've lived in New York City with a cruel and nasty step-father. Even he wasn't as threatening as that horse knocking me to the ground. It was like the horse and rider came out of nowhere."

"Shh, don't think about such things. You need to clear your mind and get better. We'll talk about it as soon as you feel good."

"I feel great standing right here on this balcony next to you."

"You're amazing, Hannah." Max turned her to him so they faced each other. He cautiously pressed his hands against her cheeks and lifted her face to his. Ever so gently, he pressed his mouth to hers. Max tried hard to keep it light because she was so fragile. He didn't expect Hannah to moan in his mouth and take her one good arm and wrap it around his neck. If they kept this up, he wouldn't need to worry about her going to sleep and falling in to a coma.

Max tightened his arms around her, pressing her whole body against his. Max had never felt this way before. Having her in his arms brought back a longing for someone to be in the center of his life. For so long he had been a loner, living a quiet life in Arizona, working the ranch, taking care of his aunt.

It made him realize he wanted more. Needed more. Something began to stir from deep within that Max had stuffed to the bottom of his core for so long.

Hannah giggled. The sound vibrated against his mouth. Reluctantly, he pulled away. "What is it, darling? What is so funny?"

She continued to smile, her eyes shining like a ray of sunshine on a cloudy day. "Business partners don't do this, Max."

"This?" he asked, bringing his face closer yet. He nipped her bottom lip with his mouth, teasing, causing her to laugh out loud. Oh, that laugh, it stirred him to his very being.

"Yes. Nor do they call their partner *darling*."

Max, careful not to cause her any pain, took her good arm, lifted her hand, kissing the inside of her palm. He placed it on his cheek and closed his eyes. "You're right. Except I am starting to believe I want it all."

"Impossible, Max. I've been thinking this through. We are both from homes where we lost our mothers. We've had horrible fathers. It's no wonder we try to find solace in each other's arms. But it won't last. What will happen if you decide to move on from here?"

"I'll take you along. You are my wife, after all."

Hannah took a step back. "I should sit down."

"Not yet. You've got to stay awake for another hour at least."

"Is this why you were kissing me, Max? To distract me and to keep me awake? Should I be ashamed for throwing myself in to your arms?"

Max pulled her close. "Never. Between a married couple, nothing is shameful."

She smiled. "Good, because I am not. I like when you kiss me."

"Then we should practice again." He pulled her tight against him, dipping his head and kissing her again like nobody's business. Hannah wrapped her arm around his neck, running her fingers through his hair. He liked how bold she was, going for what she wanted. She was the perfect business partner. He hoped to convince her they could have it all right here on this ranch. To hell with Arizona. He'd wire his aunt and let her know he was going to settle here, with Hannah. She made him feel as if he were home. Marni, Mary and even Georgie. All the rest of the stuff could go. It was overpriced art, furniture they would never use and a house that needed to be made into a home.

He would turn this small town around if it killed him.

<><>

Somewhere in the deep recesses of Hannah's mind, a voice told her to stop being so indulgent. Yet, she didn't care to stop. This euphoric feeling tugged at her until she couldn't help but to kiss Max as if he meant the world to her. He hadn't stopped her so it must be ok. He did say nothing is shameful in a marriage bed.

The thought of a perfect marriage with him was like a hard slap in the face.

This marriage was a farce. Max was keeping her busy, kissing her so she wouldn't fall in to a coma. He needed her to help turn the Ward name around. She had read about the soldiers in the war with head injuries and how they needed to keep alert. Her mail order bride business arrangement was exactly that. An arrangement. She had to force herself to push away from him.

Hannah lowered her eyes, her chin dropping to her chest. "Oh, Max. I'm so sorry. It must be the head injury. I realize we have a business arrangement. Please, forgive me for being so bold."

Strong, hard working fingers took hold of her chin, gently lifting her face to his. Dark eyes delved in to her own. "I'm not sorry. Not one bit. I plan to change your mind about our business arrangement as soon as this town accepts the fact the Wards are here to stay. I think you are safe now, Hannah, but I'll have Mary stay with you while I take care of some business." With those words, he left her there, standing on the balcony. Hannah clutched the railing, wondering what in the world had happened.

Mary came through just as Hannah turned to go inside. She helped Hannah to the settee along the wall. The two spent several hours together, talking and laughing, as Mary told her stories of how Wichita Falls came to be. Hannah realized she was being armed with information about the residents of this town by a teenager. She noted every single thing in the back of her mind. Knowing the deep, dark secrets of the townsfolk would give her more than enough information to make them realize they weren't perfect either.

For instance, Jim Wheeler. He had been an outlaw, plain and simple. Killed many men if those tales were true. He gave up his gun when a woman he fell in love with died in his arms. She had lived here in Wichita Falls. When he went after the man who hurt his true love, he gunned him down in the street. Everyone who lived here at that time turned their heads to the crime. They called it fate.

Now he ran the mercantile, resigned to stay here where his true love was buried. It was the way of the west, Mary told her.

Glancing at the door, she wondered where Max had gone. She heard voices in the hall right before Marni came in with her dinner. "Max wants you to eat in your room tonight and get some rest."

"I am getting tired. I'd like to turn in soon." The darkening sky cast the room in shadows. Mary got up and lit some oil lamps. A candle sat on either side of the oversized bed. She lit those, casting more shadows as the light from the candles flickered across the wall and ceilings.

"Don't fret, Hannah. Eat some supper and then we'll get you in a nice warm bath. After that, you should be fine to sleep all night. I'll give you a nightcap to help you sleep."

Later, after her meal and the lavender bath and a glass of Marni's special *concoction*, Hannah's eyelids became heavy. Marni and Mary helped her to bed. She pulled the covers to her chin.

"Where is Max?"

"He had to go out for a bit. Don't worry, he'll be back soon."

Hannah sighed. "I hope so. I think I want one of those goodnight kisses."

She took in a deep breath, her eyelids fluttering until they stilled.

"I think she is in love already," she heard Mary whisper to her grandmother.

"Well, then, perhaps my Max has finally found true love."

Hannah wanted to tell them both it wasn't true love. "It's a business thing," she croaked, her voice hoarse, her lips moving in directions she had no control of.

"Go to sleep, dear Hannah."

"When Max comes home, tell him, that, tell him that I -"

Max rode hell bent for leather through the prairie, pushing the stallion for all it was worth. The long-barrel rifle hung from the saddle in case he needed to use it. Max hoped he wouldn't have to but wasn't afraid, especially to some low life who tried to hurt his wife. If there was one thing he learned from his father it was no one messed with what belonged to him. Byron Ward was evil. He took what he wanted and hurt these townsfolk. Max realized all that but he'd be damned if they would reciprocate that and hurt someone who was innocent.

He was about to find the man who tried to run over his Hannah and knew exactly where to go. Max had sent Georgie to town a few hours ago. He told him when he found the culprit to sit tight, as soon as Hannah was out of danger, he would join him.

It didn't take long to spot the buck board at the saloon the moment Max rode around the corner of Main. Several horses were tied there so Max had no idea who was the man at fault. He didn't care. Sliding off the stallion, he pulled the rifle from his saddle and hit the boarded walk, the heels of his boots making a sound loud enough passers-by knew he was on a mission.

There was still some dust that rose up when he got off his horse. From the corner of his eye, Max noticed a group of four men catty-corner across the street, sitting at a make-shift table on the front porch playing cards.

One man looked up. When he noticed the shotgun slung over Max's shoulder, he nudged another man. The two rose.

"Better mind your business," Max mumbled, even though he knew it wasn't loud enough for them to hear. He pushed his way in to the saloon, adjusting his eyes to the murky light, taking in the scenery. The place was packed, several tables crowded with men drinking and playing cards.

Georgie was sandwiched in between two men at the bar. He nodded to his right, meaning the man who had attacked Hannah was right beside him. As Max began the slow walk to the front of the saloon, he noticed how the man leaned over the bar, unsteady, needing it to hold him up. He would get no satisfaction beating a drunkard.

"I'm afraid there's no shotguns allowed," the barkeep spoke up over the noisy room. The tall man built like a brick wall reached across he bar. Max tried to stare him down but the barkeep wasn't going to be intimidated.

Max shrugged and handed over the weapon. He didn't need it for the drunkard. The man was three sheets to the wind. He pushed his way in between Georgie and the drunk. Leaning closer, Max stared at the man. His head was covered in a cowboy hat, the kind that has seen better days.

"Georgie, you say this is the man who ran down my wife."

Georgie nodded then realized Max's eyes were on the drunkard. "Yes, sir. He is the one." Several men turned their heads, their chatter ceased.

The drunk laughed. "What you talking about old man? I didn't run anyone down. Prove it."

Georgie wasn't a fighting man. His nervous demeanor made Max realize he put the old guy in a compromise. But Georgie didn't back down. "I know it is true because you got the same filthy clothes on ya had earlier! I can smell ya a mile away."

Patrons of the bar began to cackle and laugh. "It's true, he is nasty smelling," someone shouted out, causing the whole bar to whoop and holler.

"I'm going to ask you real nice this time. Why'd you try to run over my wife?"

The drunk, fully awake now, raised his hands in the air. "I didn't try to hurt her. It was an accident."

"Then you admit you did it?"

Fear crossed his face. "Lookie here, I'm not a fighter. Ah hell, I ain't gonna take no blame for this."

Max suspected as much. "Who paid you to knock down my wife in the light of day?"

When the drunk took a slug of his beer, Max grabbed the glass and threw it over the bar, the mug crashing to the ground. The drunks eyes widened. "Hey, there was no call to waste a good drink."

"Woah now, fellow. Don't be doing that!" someone else yelled out.

Max glanced at the barkeep. He noticed the big man shoved the gun further back, out of Max's reach. Max didn't need to use a gun. His wit and a set of fists were all he planned on using tonight. Digging in his pockets, he retrieved a pocketful of gold coins, throwing them on the bar. "The lot goes to the first person to tell me who this clown works for?"

"I'll take that, son," an older man yelled, coming up to the bar and holding out his palm. "That'd be the South Round Ranch, right next to yours."

"Much obliged," Max answered. He motioned for the man to pick up the coins on the bar while he dug in his other pocket for more. "There's another one to give me the name of the owner of that ranch."

"No need. The owner is right here." A tall man came through the crowd, a wide-rimmed cowboy hat tilted a bit to the right. He stared at the older man picking up the money. "You're fired."

The old cowboy shrugged. "Won't be my first time, nor my last." Gathering the coins from the bar, Max put up his hand. "Come see me in the morning if you need a job."

When the cowboy disappeared, Max stood face to face with the owner of the ranch next to his. "What's your name?"

"Doesn't matter what my name is, Ward. I'm going to run you out of here and take over that ranch. Won't be long till your kind moves on."

"Yeah, get the riff-raff out of town!" someone slurred.

"Here, here!" Another yelled out. The crowd began to get rowdy.

Max's patience was wearing thin. "I figure you paid this drunkard to run over my wife. Is that right?"

Max clenched his fists when the older man nodded. He was cocky and arrogant. "Guess so but no one was supposed to get hurt. Told him to scare the lass, make her want to leave on the next train out."

"You don't know Hannah. She'll be more determined to fight you now, you arrogant son-of-a-gun." Max fumed. He raised his fist and planted it dead in the center of the man's jaw. The cowboy jerked back, stumbling for a second before he straightened up and came after Max.

After that it was an all out war in the saloon. The music stopped. Voices were raised, fists began to fly through the air, unsure of where they would land. It was a free for all, with Max pounding the cowboy with both his fists. He was not a violent man but the atmosphere, the way the cowboy acted as if he did no harm got the best of Max. A young cowboy jumped on his back before he flung him off.

Before Max knew what was happening, another landed there, knocking him to the ground. Three fists came flying at him, hitting him in the skull, his face, pummeling his shoulders and stomach. Max figured he was done for now but continued to fight, kicking and raising his fists to no avail.

Two men pulled several cowboys away, grabbed Max by the arms and drug him out of the bar. They got him on to his feet, along with two other men and practically carried him across the street. All Max remembered was a sign, something about a Land Office before it all went blank.

Chapter 6

Max stirred. Afraid to open his eyes, he figured he would see bars after the all out brawl he started. Mustering up the courage to lift heavy lids, four men, along with four beautiful women stared down at him.

"He's alive," a soft voice said, her thick blonde hair pulled back in a tight bun. She had the most beautiful creamy skin he ever laid eyes upon. A pure angel stood there, along with three other women, dark-haired, who were just as beautiful.

"Did I die? Am I in heaven?" he asked.

One of the men chuckled. "I'd say right now you are in hell, brother. I'm Marshall Montgomery. I wouldn't move any muscles if I were you."

Max tried to lift his hand. Pain shot through his arm like a hot branding iron. His other arm felt the same way. He hung his head. "I can't move. Help me up."

Marshall quipped. "You were being trampled on when we got you out of the saloon. Lucky your back isn't broken."

Two of the men helped him to a sitting position. Max was on a settee in a big room, a pot-bellied stove in the center. A large desk sat along one area, overlooking a large picture window. He tried to read the letters through the glass but found it impossible. Max ached in every bone and muscle. He tried to stand. It didn't happen.

"Now, Mr. Ward, you sit right there and settle yourself. Here's some brandy, warmed up." The one dark-haired beauty handed him a tin cup. He struggled to lift it to his mouth. She guided his hand as if he were a mere child. After taking a few large gulps, which slid down his throat and tasted mighty refreshing, he realized they knew who he was. "You called me by my name. You're not offended?"

One of the other men shook his head. "If anyone here should be, it would be me. I'm Ben Sloan, this is my wife Lily." The woman clung on to her husband's arm. She had dark hair, a beautiful smile and a worried look in her eyes.

"Ben. Lily."

One of the other ladies spoke up. "Lily is the one your father wanted, but that's another story."

Max's eyes shot up. The name rang a bell. Why were they being nice to him? Rumor had it that Lily hated his father. She had stood up to him in the end.

"I am sorry about your father, Mr. Ward."

"Max. It's Max. Maybe I should change my last name. Ward seems to bring out the worst of people in this town." Dawson and Grace Sloan introduced themselves next.

Marshall Montgomery spoke up after his wife poked him in the side. Max pretended not to notice. "This is my wife, Ruby."

"Pleased to meet you, Max."

Max nodded, turning to the other man standing beside Marshall.

"I'm Daniel Ashwood. I believe we met the other night. I was closed. This is my wife, Charity."

He nodded to the couple. The two were even now giving each other a look that made Max yearn for Hannah. "I need to get back to my ranch." He tried to stand. A pain shot through his hip and thigh that made him groan out loud.

Marshall hauled him up on his feet, while Ben and Dawson each slung an arm over their shoulder. "Your hired hand is waiting with the buck board. We'll get you there and ride with you back to your ranch. Just in case there's some shenanigans going on. We heard the South Round Ranch is after your land. Everyone is fired up tonight. Best we give you a hand."

"I'm not sure why you even care, but, thank you. I can get home myself."

The women tsked, tsked, and shook their heads in unison.

"It ain't gonna happen, my friend." Dawson's voice rose above the women. "You can barely walk let alone get on that stallion. Lucky for you we just happened to be having our weekly card game tonight."

He was right. Looks like he made some friends. Who knew a saloon brawl would weed them out.

Max, determined to ride on the hard seat with Georgie, bounced around, teetering back and forth. His stallion was tied to the buck board, following behind while the four riders rode two on each side of the wagon.

The ride back to the ranch went well with no surprises. The four men hauled Max inside to Marni's cry of dismay. They got him as far as the settee in the parlour when he collapsed. "I'm fine, dammit. Just need to take a rest here." Then he immediately passed out.

<> <>

Hannah stirred when she heard the loud noises outside her room right before the door was flung open. Her head felt so much better after resting for hours. Gasping at the commotion, she pushed the covers back, jumping from her bed to stand on the cool floor in her bare feet.

Four men carried Max, his bruised and bloody body to her bed.

She gasped and slapped a hand over her mouth so she didn't cry out.

"Ma'am, sorry to disturb you."

"Put him in the bed," one of the men ordered.

Marni came bustling in to the room. "That wasn't exactly the right bed, but, well, just put him there anyway."

Hannah watched the scene play out before her. She finally found her voice. "What happened?"

Marni rushed to her side, placing a robe over her shoulders. Hannah let the robe warm her. She gathered the material closer.

"Sorry to disturb you, Mrs. Ward. Seems your husband got in to a fight. He'll be fine, just needs some tending to."

"A fight? Why?"

"I can't answer that. We should go." The tall man, the spokesperson of the group turned to the others. Hannah watched him mouth to the others that they should leave. Probably before she asked too many questions.

"Thank you for bringing him home. Can we get you anything?"

"No. Were fine, we'll be on our way."

"Marni, please see them out."

When everyone left, Hannah stood by the bed, staring down at Max. His eye was swelled, his nose bloody and scratches covered his face. She gazed at his hands, the knuckles swelled and bleeding. It reminded her of the boxer friends her step-father would bet on. They were a brutal bunch. What in the world was Max doing getting in to a fight?

She poured water in to a basin from the pitcher on her night stand, tore a sheet in pieces and began the task of washing his face. He winced but she kept on until every spot of blood disappeared. Hannah busied herself cleaning his bruised knuckles, washing each finger and carefully wrapping a sheet of linen around his hand. When she was finished she looked up to find his eyes on her.

Max tried to speak. His voice was gravely, strained. "Thank you."

She placed a hand against his cheek. "You took care of me, remember. Not even twenty-four hours ago. What happened?"

He winced. "I believe I got whooped."

She smiled. "By the looks of your hand, I believe you did a bit of whooping yourself."

"There were too many of them," he mumbled, his eyes closing.

"How many were there?" she asked, her heart pounding.

"A saloon full."

Her hand stilled. "What? You took on a whole saloon full of men?"

He groaned. "Something like that."

Hannah remembered the man on the horse that ran her over had gone in to the saloon. "Oh, Max, did you go after that man? The one who tried to hurt me?"

"Hmm," was the only thing that came from his mouth. Hannah watched the steady rhythm of his chest as he fell in to a deep sleep. Marni came in to check on them but left after seeing Hannah had everything under control.

The four men who brought him home had put him in the wrong bed. Determined to make the best of things, Hannah doused the lamps and climbed in beside Max. She pulled the covers over their bodies and laid on her back, feeling the heat from his. Snuggling closer, she let her mind drift, knowing the events of the day meant the two of them were more than just business partners. It was happening so fast. She wanted more than a casual business relationship with him and now it seemed to be going in that direction.

She had the right to be sleeping in the same bed as her husband. Then why did she feel as if she was doing something wrong? She was married to him, for life. There was no way they could make a business relationship work for the rest of their lives. Not when every fiber of her being called out to his. Not when being near him caused every single nerve in her body to stand on end.

Max moaned in his sleep, turned and flung an arm across her stomach. His touch scorched her skin, sending Hannah to snuggle even closer. A need she had never before realized filled her up. Before she knew what hit her, Max nestled his face in her neck, his warm breath sending shivers down her spine.

"Oh." She didn't understand the fires that were burning inside of her. A strange feeling began low in her belly, below his hand. No one had ever made her feel this way before. Hannah didn't understand, found it confusing. She tried to move away from his hand, his burning touch but he held on to her.

"No. Stay." His words caused her to gasp. The warmth tickled the skin on her neck and she pushed in, wanting to feel it again. Max's mouth began to move slowly, pressing kisses there, drifting lower, at the neckline of her gown. A groan escaped him from somewhere deep in his throat.

Hannah tried to touch him but her arm was caught under her, the other in a sling. She let her head fall back so he could kiss her neck where she exposed the skin. It felt so right, so exquisite she wasn't sure how to come back from this euphoria.

Then it stopped. She heard his breath rising and falling in unison to realize he was sleeping. Her body ached for something she had no clue of. But then a small smile crept upon her face. He had gone to the saloon to fight for her honor. No one had ever done that. She always had to fight her own battles. Interesting.

Hannah yawned. It had been a heck of a day. First, getting run over by a careless rider and then this, her husband, acting like a knight in shining armor. She turned her head and placed a gentle kiss on his brow, letting her lips linger there for a brief moment.

Hannah closed her eyes. Could she be falling in love with this man?

<> <> <>

Hannah woke to find an empty bed. As she got dressed, her eye caught his profile sitting out on her balcony, his back to her. She slid out of the door to come up behind him. Placing her hands on his shoulder, she leaned down and kissed him on the cheek. He winced.

"How are you feeling this morning, Max?" Hanna sat down in the opposite chair, noticing he had a tray with a cup of coffee for her. She busied herself with the pot, pouring herself a cup and refilling Max's cup. Sipping on the warm liquid, she waited for an answer.

"Sore. My ego is bruised."

"Must've been quite some fight." She was smiling.

He shook his head. "I went in there after one man. Didn't realize the whole saloon would start brawling."

"Lucky for you those men brought you back here."

"Yeah, guess not everyone hates the Ward name. Reminds me, I need to go thank them today."

"I think perhaps you should stay out of town for awhile. At least until the bruises heal."

He rubbed his jaw. "You're right. No sense in letting them see all the damage they did to me." Max leaned his head back.

"Hannah, I'm not sure I can fix things. No one wants to hear the Ward name. Everyone and I mean everyone, hated my father. That's a big burden to carry."

Hannah's heartstrings tugged at his words. "Not everyone. The men who brought you back here seemed to care. Start with them." She reached across and took his hand. "Max, we'll do this together. I have some ideas I'd like to share with you."

He turned his head slightly, wincing as he did so. "I like you, Hannah. More so than I ever thought I would care about anyone. When you got knocked over by the horse and rider, I lost my mind, my anger got the best of me. I went after that man planning to hurt him but good. We've got a good thing going here, I hate to lose that."

"Why would we lose that? I don't understand."

"I brought you here on a business arrangement. If we can't turn this town around, I'll understand if you want to go back to New York."

Hannah got up to kneel down in front of him. She took both hands in hers. "Maximilian Ward, I'm ashamed of you, giving up after one silly saloon fight."

He gazed at her with dark eyes so intense it surprised her. "I'm not giving up. I care about you and don't want anything to happen." He took her hand and brought it to his mouth.

"Max."

"I won't let anyone hurt you again. This whole thing, the reason I'm here. It's not worth anything if you get hurt."

"That's the sweetest thing anyone has ever said to me. Thank you."

"I mean those words. I won't hold you to this marriage if you want out."

Hannah panicked. Was he trying to get rid of her? "I wasn't planning on going anywhere, Max."

He grinned. "Good. I don't want you to go."

"Do you mean that? Truly?"

"Truly."

"There for a moment I thought it was your way of getting rid of me."

He shook his head. Wrapped his arm around her and pulled her forward. "Never," he mumbled right before catching her mouth with his own.

The kiss was sweet, meaningful. As if he were claiming her. She gave back from deep in her core, showing him that she meant every word she said. When they broke apart, he held her, words not necessary.

Hannah looked up at him. "I know this was supposed to be all about a business arrangement, Max. I want to try to make it a real marriage. I'll never go back to New York. My life is here, with you. Please, don't ever mention that place again."

"Deal."

"Deal, then. Let's go over my plans."

His brow shot up. A smile crept across his face. "You are taking the bull by the horns here? Well, then, tell me your ideas."

Over coffee, Hannah explained how a live auction would get people out here to the ranch.

"I don't see how it will change anyone's mind about us."

"Max, of course it will. The money from all of this stuff will be donated to build a school. Wichita Falls doesn't have one. We can hire a school teacher, too. You've got the money to do so."

He chuckled. "Spending my money so freely?"

She grinned. "Yes, I am and if you know what's good for you, you'll agree. This is the perfect way to get people here to meet you, to see you are not an evil man like he was. It will work. It has to."

Two wagons came rolling in as they were discussing the sale of almost every piece of furniture. After realizing how much Max wanted to be rid of it all, she was starting to feel a bit overwhelmed. "Can we keep our beds to sleep in?"

Max laughed as he went out the door to see who was coming in the wagons. Hannah followed to find four couples disembarking. The ladies all ran to her, giving her hugs and introducing themselves.

"I'm Ruby," the dark haired lady said. She looked very pregnant. "This will be my second child."

Hannah heard the pride in her voice. "Congratulations."

"I'm Lily."

"I'm Grace. Pleased to meet you." She held out her hand.

"I'm Charity. Co-owner of the only newspaper in Wichita Falls."

Marni came bustling out with Mary in the rear. "Come inside, Ladies. I've put tea and coffee on and some special treats."

Hannah glanced back to find Max in the middle of a serious conversation with the four men. He looked up in time to give her a nod as she followed everyone inside. A warm feeling went through her. Finally, a few friendly faces.

<> <> <>

"It's been quite awful for you, hasn't it?" Lily asked.

"I'm just thankful that all of you have come through to realize we are nothing like Byron Ward."

"Lily knows first hand and told us we have to make the first move." Grace smiled. She was always outspoken, matter of fact and got straight to the point.

"Either way, thank you. It's a relief. Now if I can figure out how to pull off this auction, I think it's another step in the right direction."

"Do tell?" Ruby said, rubbing her belly.

"Max can't stand all this furniture and art sitting here, wasting away, so I suggested we have a live auction and donate the proceeds to build a school."

"That's a great idea," Ruby told her. The others nodded in agreement.

Hannah bit her lip. "I just, I am overwhelmed. Max only wants to keep a few pieces. I don't know where to start, how to set things up. I had no idea he wanted to get rid of everything!"

Grace stood up and clapped her hands. "Oh, sweetie, you let me handle this one. I'm an accountant, by the way. This is perfect. I can do an inventory and organize it all for you. Easy peasy! Right, ladies? We can do this."

Hannah's heart swelled at the offers. She wasn't about to turn them down. "I would appreciate your help."

"We can all help. I'll write up the advertisement right away and disperse them all over town." Charity whipped out a pencil and paper from the pocket of her dress.

"Ruby and I can sell food to add to the coffers. It will be fun."

Two hours later, Max and Hannah stood waving goodbye to their new friends. Max wrapped his arm around her waist. Hannah sighed, leaned in to him. "I was worried about pulling this off alone. Now, I don't have to."

"The men are going to help the day of the auction. Marshall said one of his ranch hands is willing to act as auctioneer. He can roll his words and get the crowd going. I just hope we have a crowd."

"No worries. Grace is making a list of all the well-to-do ranch owners in the territory. She is getting their invitations ready the moment she gets back. Lily said that her and Ben know a lot of important people who stayed at their hotel. She's going to wire them about the sale. We are so lucky to have these people as friends."

Max turned, gathering her in his arms. "I'd say I'm lucky to have found you." He dipped his head to kiss her. She stood on her tip-toes and wrapped her arms around his neck.

"It looks like things are turning around for us, Mr. Ward."

"It sure does, Mrs. Ward."

Hannah kissed him back with all the muster of a wife who was starting to fall in love with her husband.

Chapter 7

The day of the sale, Max looked over his land. Everything was set up to run smoothly for the next few hours. The women worked hard, setting up tables of baked goods and food to feed the expected crowd. Even Doc Smith showed up to offer support.

Miss Addie, local proprietor of the town's only boarding house, gathered her skirts in her hand and walked up to him. She nodded and smiled, her head tipped slightly. "Mr. Ward, I'm at your service. What can I do?"

"Miss Addie, thank you for coming. Why don't you go see if the ladies need any help?"

"Of course. I'm afraid there are rumors some of the townsfolk plan to boycott the auction. You may even get a crowd of nay-sayers when the bidding starts. Be on the lookout." She swirled her skirts and went to look for the ladies. Good to know someone had their back.

Max strolled over to where Marshall and Ben were helping to set up the auction block. "Got word from Miss Addie there may be trouble later."

Ben looked up. "We'll be ready if they start trouble this time."

"Much obliged, Ben."

A whistle from the train pulling in to the depot at Wichita Falls echoed faintly across the prairie. There would be several men on that train with lots of cash money. Daniel and Dawson took a buggy to the train depot earlier to escort them back to the auction site. It had all been arranged, thanks to Grace and her skills of event planning.

Max feared the angry townsfolk who were stubborn as the day is long would try to stop the proceedings. That's why he had his ranch hands surround the auction area in case anything went awry. The men had two flags, one red, one yellow. If the yellow flag went up, it meant those who were arriving were considered safe. If the red flag went up, every available man was to get to that area. Hopefully, this way they could avoid another brawl.

Except right before the bidding began, a crowd of men, mostly from the saloon, guns in holsters on their hips and walking across the prairie as if they alone would stop the event, tried to get through the lower area. As soon as the red flag went up, every cowboy on the Ward Ranch lined up to make a barrier to keep them from entering.

"Folks, looks like there's some trouble brewing down at the southern end," the auctioneer's bold, loud voice rang out. He tried to continue with the bidding to no avail. Everyone watched the commotion.

"Yeah, it looks like the South Round Ranch hands are mad as all get out!"

Max growled. It was time the owner of the South Round stopped using these men as his lackeys. He marched up to the line and pushed his way through.

Marshall warned him. "Max, be careful. No sense in getting your butt kicked twice now."

"Don't worry, I know you got my back," he shot back. He faced the crowd. "I assume you all work for the South Round Ranch. Is that right?"

Nods followed. "What's it to ya!" one of the men yelled through the crowd.

"Aren't you sick and tired of being bullied by the owner? Making you come after me and try to intimidate someone who could pay you twice the wages that no-gooder does." Max had found out through one of his ranch hands what they got paid. It was pathetic and why he had several of the South Round hands on his payroll.

"Whaddya mean, twice the wages?"

"Yeah, I wanta know, too." The crowd of men inched their way closer.

Max stood his ground. "I'm in need of more hands. I'd pay you twice the amount you make now. A bed, food and a decent wage." Max figured from experience once these men got paid better they'd be more pleasant to work around. They needed someone to respect them, guide them and offer them a good life.

"Yeah? When can I start?"

"Right now."

One of the younger ones hollered out. "How do we know you ain't just telling us this so we don't bring trouble to your auction."

Max turned to him. "Because I am not a lying, cheating, stealing man. I'm honest and expect you to be, too. Ask any of my men here. I expect an honest days work from each and every one of you." He reached in his pocket, prepared for this. "I'll give each man an advance on his pay to come work for me right now, to help with the auction."

Every single man stepped forward. Max grinned as he handed each one a small satchel and shook their hand to welcome them to the Ward Ranch. Max knew he was taking a chance they may run back to their old boss, but he didn't really have another option. Most men understood money. He turned to see Hannah watching, along with every other person close by. When the last man took his satchel, he saw her take a deep breath and clap her hands. *Well done,* she mouthed.

"Let's get this show on the road!" a strong voice boomed over top the crowd. The auctioneer began his rattling and the auction was back in full force. Max sauntered over to where Hannah stood, her hands out to catch his. She placed a kiss on his cheek.

"You can do better than that," he told her, swinging her around and leaning her back. He commenced to kiss the daylights out of her right there while the others were paying attention to the auction.

When he let her up, she gasped for air. "Oh, my!" Her hand went to her chest. "Maximilian Ward! That was, why, that was fabulous," and she laughed out loud.

Her laughter died out when a voice, out of the blue, said something to her to make her eyes widen in disbelief.

"Well, well, well, if it isn't Hannah girl."

Hannah fainted in Max's arms.

<> <> <>

Hannah stirred awake on the porch swing. She felt it rock back and forth but when she looked down, her feet were curled under her. Max was right beside her, giving her strength with his arm across her shoulder, holding her. "What happened?"

"You fainted dead away, darling."

The reality of seeing her step-father started to come back to her. "Oh, Max. He found me."

Max pulled her closer. "Who found you? Hannah, I know things have been traumatic for you lately and with a head injury, perhaps you should go to the house. This may be too much for you."

She sat up, looking desperately around for her step-father's face. When she tried to stand, Max held her back. "No, Hannah, stop. This isn't good for you. Sit here for awhile until your head clears."

"I'm fine, Max. I just saw my step-father. He's here. How in the world did he get here?" Hannah looked in the general area where they stood earlier but he was nowhere in sight. Where did he go? Was she going crazy? She shook her head. "I am certain it was him. I'll never forget that voice."

"There is a lot of people here today. Many of them are strangers to the area. They've come in from other towns by carriage and train." Max got up from the swing. "Listen, Hannah, I want you to be able to enjoy yourself today. I've got to go check on everything but I want you to promise me you will stay right here on the swing until I return. Then, we will go together."

"You're probably right. Things have been hectic with getting ready for the sale and all."

"Good. I'll be back in a short while. You stay put. Promise me?"

She nodded. Max leaned over and raised her chin with a finger, kissing her lightly. His mouth lingered for a moment. "You are really starting to mean a lot to me, darling."

Hannah sighed. She lifted her hand and placed it over his. "I feel the same way."

"Then it's settled. Stay here and wait for me. Your one true love."

Hannah blinked. "What did you say?" she whispered, a catch in her throat.

He shrugged. "It's true, Hannah, I am sure we were meant for each other. I am in love with you."

Hannah blushed. She opened her mouth to speak but no words came out.

He placed a kiss right on her mouth. "Shh, don't say anything."

Her heart was filled with so much adoration for her husband. "Don't you want to know how I feel?"

He turned towards the crowd, then looked back and grinned, so wide, she blushed again. "I already know, darling. See you in a bit."

Hannah's heart was in her throat. She stared after him, surprised and fascinated by her husband. He was handsome and one of a kind. This business arrangement was sure turning out to be quite the turn around from a few days ago.

After boredom set in, Hannah ached to go back to the women's table, where they were selling baked goods. Unable to sit still, she stood in an effort to relieve her boredom. Part of her wanted to get back to work, yet, she remembered her promise to Max. He had asked her to stay right where she was.

Would she be a dutiful wife and stay put or wander up to the baked goods table to help the ladies who worked diligently to make this a success? Feeling as if she were letting the ladies down, she peeked around the corner to see where Max had run off to. She saw him at the auction block watching the proceedings. Lifting her arm up, she tried to get his attention. After a few moments, he looked her way.

She waved. He nodded and started towards her. She took a few steps down to meet him halfway when someone took hold of her arm and twisted. Turning to see who had grabbed a hold of her, she screamed when the face of her step-father came in to view.

"Hush, now, Hannah girl. I ain't here to harm you."

"Let my arm go."

He did.

Hannah turned to see where Max was. She didn't want to face her step-father alone.

"Who ya lookin' for? That husband of yours? No worries, my partner is keeping him busy."

Hannah jerked her head towards the auctioneer to see Max talking with one of the men who came in on the train. He was dapper with a fine three piece suit, a tall hat and cane with an ivory handle. "That man looks too fancy to be with the likes of you."

"Now that ain't no way to talk to your step-daddy. He ain't no fancier than I am. Had to find me a new line of work since you done run off and left me high and dry."

"You're a grown man. No reason you can't work for a living," Hannah told him. She crossed her arms and tilted her chin in the air. When she looked at him thoroughly, she noticed he was worn out from years of drinking. His pale skin was gray, like he didn't have much oxygen left in his lungs. Skinny as a bean pole, his clothes were so baggy she wondered how he kept his pants up.

The thought made her giggle.

"Now what you laughing at?"

"You, Richard. I won't embarrass you as to why but I will tell you this. You had better get out of here and out of my life. Why are you here?"

"No need to get rambunctious."

"Why. Are. You. Here?"

"I am in need of some cash."

"I don't have any cash. My husband does and I'll bet you already know that."

"You don't have any cash?"

"No. You took it all, remember? When you busted in to my bedroom and stole every single thing I earned."

"You owed me! I took care of you!" His voice rose. Max looked over just as she turned her head. She was desperate to get his attention.

He moved so quick, she didn't have time to blink. Before Richard could get another word out, Max was right there, his arm around her. "Is this your step-father?"

"Yes. He is trying to extort money, I'm sure."

"I didn't ask you for a penny."

Hannah huffed. "You were about to. He said he was in need of cash."

"You best be on your way." Max didn't argue the point.

"Well, that may be a problem."

"Why is that?"

"I, uh, spent all I had to get here thinking my step-daughter would be kind enough to take me in."

"No way! Why would you even think I would take you in after all you've done!"

"Now just wait here, young lady. I took care of you after your mama died, rest her soul. It was me. No one else. Has it ever occured to you I may have put you out after she was gone? But, I didn't, no sir. I took care of you."

"I took care of myself. I worked twelve hours a day in the factory, remember? Gave you every penny I had except for the little bit I hid in order to leave you for good." Max placed a hand on her cheek and turned her face to his. His look of empathy for what she had to do gave her the strength to throw her step-father off their land. Turning back to her step-father, she told him, "It's time for you to leave, Richard. Go with your rich friend and get off Ward land." Hannah knew Max approved from the way he squeezed her shoulder.

"That ain't my friend. He's a business associate."

"He is a curator at the Library of Congress who is scouting for fine art," Max mentioned. "The Library bought over fifty thousand dollars worth of my father's paintings."

Alarm bells went off in Hannah's brain. How would Richard know someone of that caliber? "Has he shown you his credentials?"

Max shrugged. "A man's word is his honor, Hannah."

She turned and began to high-step it towards the man in the fancy suit. "Not for a thief, it isn't."

"Wait, Hannah!"

When she came face to face with the man, she recognized him instantly. "You!" It was indeed a cohort of Richards.

The man's eyes got round as saucers. She pointed a finger at him. "This man is a fraud! He has no money."

The man looked affronted but Hannah knew better. She spent too many nights listening to the two before they went off to gamble her pay check away.

Max stood beside her. "Is this true, Mr. Remington?"

Hannah placed a hand on her hip. "Remington! That man's name is Smithton. Martin Smithton, the worst con artist in the vicinity of New York City. What happened, Mr. Smithton, did they run you out of town?" Hannah was impressed with her ability to stand up to these men. They had intimidated her for way too long. She looked over at Max, who was staring the man down. It felt wonderful to have someone by her side who believed in her.

"My wife says you are a fraud. I assume your payment is also."

He pulled a letter of intent from his pocket. Hannah leaned over. "It's also fake. There is no Mulberry Bank in existence any longer. It closed down a year before I ever left New York City. I know, I removed my money right before it did."

"How do you know? You never put your money in a bank. It was all hidden in the wall of your bedroom!" Richard stood beside his cohort now, facing Max, Hannah and several others who wondered over to listen.

Max stiffened beside her when she said, "Becky's father worked there. I knew it was shutting down thanks to my friend. I withdrew my money and hid it in the wall, until you found it and stole every single penny!"

Max reached out to grab the older man's shirt front, but stopped when she cried out. "It's not worth the trouble, Max."

He stopped himself. Instead, he took the check and ripped it into tiny pieces. Max stepped forward, opened the fancy pocket and stuffed the worthless pieces of paper inside. "Get off my property. I'm going to count to ten. If you are not gone, I'll shoot you both."

"Here, you may need this." Marshall Montgomery stood beside him, his outstretched hand holding a pistol. When the two con-men saw he did indeed have a real gun, they took off like bats out of their cave, not looking back.

Hannah held a hand over her mouth but her giggles couldn't be helped.

Max flung an arm over her shoulder. "They look quite comical running like that."

Hannah nodded. "If this weren't so serious, I'd tend to agree. Where will they go?"

"I could care less. Let the wolves eat their carcass for all I care. After what that man did to you, I don't care what he does." Max wrapped his other arm around her, heedless to the many stares their way.

"I think they are too close. They are dirty little buggers, Max. I know him. He'll come back. Maybe hide a day or two first. I just want him far away from here."

Max looked in to her eyes. Hannah had never asked him for anything before but she needed this. She wanted no part of her step-fathers shenanigans, ever again. Her step-father reminded her of all the damage he had done over the years. "He worked my mother to the bone, caused her to have an early death. I was headed that way myself."

"Hannah." Max kissed her mouth. The crowd around them got silent. She didn't hear the auctioneer in the background or the people mingling around. Max was kissing her as if there was no one else in the vicinity. As if she meant the world to him. As if he loved her.

When he pulled back, she smiled up at him. "I love you, Max."

He grinned. "I know."

She swatted his arm as he turned to one of the men close by. "Gather those two idiots up and get them on a train today to the east. Make sure they have a one way ticket there. Don't come back until you can tell me they are gone."

"Max, that's too kind of you. But, it isn't right. They got away with trying to steal from you. What is the punishment here?"

He gathered Hannah back in his arms. "I'll send a wire to my aunt. She has quite the collection of admirers, one of which is the commissioner of the police department in the city of New York. She travels there every year to go shopping. Trust me, they won't make it two feet from the train depot until someone stops them."

A sigh of relief escaped Hannah. "Thank you. I owe you so much."

"You owe me nothing, Hannah."

Hannah ignored his comment. She did owe him so much. She was going to be the best wife ever. Instead, she asked, "When will I get to meet this aunt of yours, Max? She sounds wonderful."

"She is. Did you know she is a singer? She has traveled all over the country and as far away as Paris in her heyday."

"She doesn't sing any longer?"

He shook his head. "I'm afraid not. Something happened in Dallas. She suddenly left the stage and never looked back. I'm afraid she lost her voice after that, claiming she can no longer sing and hasn't been able to get back up on stage ever since."

"I'm so sorry. Still, I'd love to meet her."

"She has found a haven at the ranch in Arizona. Hasn't left it in five years. I've made sure she is quite comfortable there. When I wire her, I'll ask her to come for a visit and why. I didn't tell her yet that I married."

Hannah stepped back. "You haven't told her?"

"I'm afraid not. It was a spur of the moment idea. One that I only decided when I got here."

The auctioneer concluded the sale and wished everyone a pleasant day, offering baked goods at a special price at the ladies table. Clapping began slowly and then the crowd went wild as the spirit of the day overcame everyone at once.

Max grinned. Hannah smiled. Arm in arm they were greeted by townsfolk who apologized for treating them badly. Women went out of their way to welcome Hannah to the town of Wichita Falls. Slaps on the back for Max went on and on.

"It seems people are having a change of heart," Max told her.

She nodded. "Of course. How could they not, Mr. Ward. You alone have turned this town on its toes. Now go grab the auctioneers stand before they tear it down and make your announcement."

"I was never alone, Hannah Ward. We did it together." Max took a deep bow and when he rose his amused eyes caught hers. Promises of something wonderful shone in them. Hannah took a breath and held it, realizing that they would have a real marriage, not in name only.

This marriage was never a business arrangement. Not from the very beginning. A slow smile spread across Hannah's face as she watched her husband announce the idea of a schoolhouse for the town.

Chapter 8

Six months later

The hotel lobby was decorated to the hilt. Everyone in town was gathered there to celebrate the newly built schoolhouse. Hannah and Max stood by the food table, enjoying the proceedings. Hand shakes and slaps on the back from every man in town had Max grumbling and exhausted.

"I'm never building another thing again," he complained.

"Honey, they are happy you didn't turn out to be your father. From the stories being circulated, he was a man of no remorse."

"I'm glad it is all over. My back has been slapped over and over again and it's feeling pretty sore right now."

Hannah placed an arm around his waist then slowly began to rub his back. "Perhaps after this is all over, I may take some of that magic oil I got from Lu's speciality shop and make it feel all better."

The look he gave her made her smile. "Magic oil?"

Hannah blushed. "Lu invited me back to her store the other day when I was visiting Grace. She apologized for treating me so badly the first time I came to town and gave me some items to try, courtesy of her establishment."

"Let's get out of here."

She laughed out loud. "We can't. Your aunt is due. Any moment the train will arrive."

He nuzzled her ear. "Can't say I didn't try. What else did you acquire at Lu's shop?"

"She gave me some bath soaps in lavender scents and some other bottles of oils."

"Darling, we have to get out of here."

Hannah kissed him on the cheek. "I'm going to go help the ladies. Lily and Grace have been doing most of the hostessing. Thank you for bringing me here, Max. I have friends I can rely on and a husband who adores me."

Max grinned. "I will do more than adore you. Let's get out of here. We can come back later."

She titled her head before shaking it back and forth. "Behave, husband. I'm not sure what to do with all this attention you bestow upon me."

Before he could say a word, the door of the hotel swung open and it seemed as if the air swirled around the beautiful creature who practically swayed back and forth as she entered the room.

The lobby was like a grand entrance for her. Hannah stared in fascination as Max's aunt glided through the door, a gown of exquisite material unlike any other seen in the small town of Wichita Falls. "Maximilian!" she squealed, her skirts bouncing as she hurried to his side. She grabbed his cheeks and kissed each one before turning to Hannah.

"You must be Hannah, darling." Her voice, so lovely, so soft, rang out over the hushed crowd.

"Welcome," Hannah said, holding out her hand. She wanted to curtsey, the woman was almost like royalty, that's how grand she seemed.

"Come here, child," she sang, taking Hannah in her arms and giving her a big hug. "Welcome to the Ward family. Maximilian has told me so much about you."

"Oh?"

She nodded. "Yes, he has told me how beautiful you are and how much he loves and adores you. That is all I need to know. He's right, you are beautiful."

Hannah blushed. "Thank you. That is an honor coming from someone who is so beautiful herself." Hannah was sure people told her she was beautiful more often than not.

"Let me introduce you to my friends." Max moved his aunt through his new circle of friends, trying hard to include everyone. It seemed to Hannah he found his place in this small town, the one that had rebuked him at first.

She sighed. It was going to be a great life here in Wichita Falls. Perhaps her step-father did her a favor after all. She would never know this town or the people if he hadn't gotten greedy and taken her stash of money.

"What's the secretive smile all about?" a gentle voice interrupted her private thoughts.

"Hi Miss Addie. You look lovely, as always."

Miss Addie held two cups of punch. She handed Hannah one and stood beside her watching the crowd enjoying the party. "Thank you, Hannah. You are happy with Mr. Ward?"

She nodded. "Bliss, Miss Addie. He has given me a reason to live. I hated life with my step-father but felt stuck. I'm glad my friend Becky left the newspaper on my night stand that day."

"So am I. Looks like I'll cross another success story off my list."

Hannah stared at Miss Addie. "What did you have to do with this?" She knew Addie did some matchmaking, yet had no idea she was involved. "How do you take credit for Max and I?"

Miss Addie lifted her chin and smiled. "Child, I have connections all over the frontier, from California to New York City to Boston to Chicago. The mail order brides that come to Wichita Falls are no accident. We are building one of the finest towns in the West, my dear. You are a part of history in the making."

"Do you mean to tell me you know Aloisa? Hers was the agency where I applied."

"I made it my job to know all of the main matchmaking companies in the big cities and even in some that are not so well-known. My credentials for finding a perfect match are untouched, Hannah. Trust me, you were always in good hands. There are some services that do not investigate thoroughly and the results are not so good."

"Then I can be reassured my friend Becky has found a good match. She went through Aloisa's services, also."

Hannah heard Miss Addie's breath hitch. "I'm afraid not, Hannah. I had nothing to do with that match. There has been some speculation that the man out right lied. When she got to her destination, someone there warned your friend ahead of time. She took action and didn't marry the man."

"Oh dear, this is awful. I'm afraid she may be in trouble then?"

"No. She's not in a dire situation. I believe Aloisa found out about her dire straits and found her a place to stay until she can find her another match."

"She would love it here in Wichita Falls." Hannah scanned the crowd. "What about him?" She pointed to a tall, dark, handsome loner.

"Him?"

She nodded. "Yes. I hear he's going to be our new sheriff? That's if the committee agrees unanimously."

Miss Addie pressed her finger to her chin, puckering her ruby red lips as she pondered. "Rumors are he's got a bit of a wild side."

Hannah leaned over and whispered in Addie's ear. "My husband is kinda wild. You picked him for me."

"Good point. Well, I do believe you may have something here, Hannah. To have your best friend married to the sheriff would be an ideal situation. It would help to save Aloise's reputation as well if we can find a perfect match for Rebecca."

"It would be the best ever."

"I better get to work then," Addie mentioned, setting her cup of punch on the table behind them.

"Tonight? Why not enjoy the party."

"My work is never done." A three piece band struck up a slow ballad. Miss Addie twisted her way through the crowd until she came to the town's almost newly appointed sheriff. "Sir, would you care to dance?"

Hannah watched in amazement as the dark-haired man bowed to the lovely Miss Addie, treating her with a kind smile and twirling her around the room. She smiled, hope deep in her heart. It would be wonderful if her friend married someone in Wichita Falls.

"I'm ready to go home now." Her husbands warm breath tickled her ear.

"Are you now? Where is your dear aunt?"

"Over there. She is the limelight of many single men tonight. She wants to stay so I got her a room here at the hotel."

Hannah was surprised. "She doesn't want to stay at the ranch?"

"Not at all." He laughed out loud. "My aunt wants to be the center of attention. She says she can't be stuck on a ranch with lonely old cowboys who have no idea who she is."

"I thought she was living on a ranch in Arizona as a recluse?"

"I think this trip has changed her somehow. Brought her back to the life she knew before hiding away at the ranch. This will be good for her. For us, too, darling. I want you all to myself."

Hannah turned in his arms, placing her hands around his neck. "All seems to be settled here, husband. Let's go home."

"I can't wait for you to rub that oil all over me."

"Shush, you'll start rumors."

"How can they be rumors when it's all true."

Hannah giggled. "Don't move. I'll be right back as soon as I say good-bye to the ladies."

She looked back once to see those dark eyes staring at her. Hannah winked at him, drawing a look that burned her to her core. It was going to be a sweet night with the husband of her dreams. Who knew when she started out on this trek she would find a husband like Max Ward.

Hugs and kisses followed her out the door as everyone wished them goodnight. Hannah and Max walked hand in hand to the buggy. As he helped her up, Max brushed a hand over her backside. One of the older ladies outside left out a shocked sound that made Max laugh out loud.

Hannah blushed. "Max, stop teasing. That poor woman will have heart palpitations."

He got up beside her on the bench. With a jerk of his wrist, the buggy was off, heading to the ranch they called home.

"I love you for always, Max Ward. I'm so glad you were the one."

He kissed her.

"Aren't you going to say you love me?"

Max gave her that smile, the one that melted her heart. "You already know I do, Mrs. Ward. Now it's time to show you how much."

Hannah grinned. It was going to be a wonderful life.

*****

Thank you for reading Max and Hannah's story. Next up in the lives of the townsfolk of Wichita Falls is Becky's story. Rebecca thought she had found true love as a mail order bride. She had been writing back and forth for months to a wonderful sounding gentleman with two kids and a farm. He proclaimed to need help but when she got to her destination, to her horror, he had lied through his rotting teeth.

Now, she was stuck in a strange town, hiding from a horrible man until Aloisa's Matchmaking Agency found someone else to help her. Now available on Amazon. Follow the link below....

Rebecca: Mail Order Brides of Wichita Falls Series - Book 6[1]
(http://amzn.to/2nbgRkz)
Available Now...[2] (http://amzn.to/2nbgRkz)

Do you like to read all 8 stories in one shot?
Get Volume 1
Box Set Available Now on Amazon[3] (https://www.amazon.com/
gp/product/B076YXYBN8)

---

1. http://amzn.to/2nbgRkz

2. http://amzn.to/2nbgRkz

3. https://www.amazon.com/gp/product/B076YXYBN8

Cyndi Rayes Books

Books by Cyndi Raye
    Mail Order Brides of Wichita Falls Series
    Ruby
    Grace
    Lily
    Charity
    Hannah
    Rebecca
    Sophie
    Ellie
    Jenna
    Leila
    Boxed Set Vol 1-8
    Voume 2 - Vol 9-11 (with Addie's Final Chapter)
    Christmas in Wichita Falls Holiday Book
    Brides of Mill Ridge Series
    An Outlaws Honor
    A Reverend's Rose
    The Ranger's Redemption
    A Doctor's Devotion
    A Teacher's Treasure
    A Sister's Sanctuary
    Sons of Nora White Series
    A Bride for Luke
    A Bride for Adam
    A Bride for Samuel
    A Groom for Nora

A Bride for Russell
A Bride for Wesley
A Groom for Widow Young
Multi-Author Series Contributions
A Bride for Abel - The Proxy Brides
A Bride for Calvin - The Proxy Brides
A Bride for Arthur - The Proxy Brides
An Agent for Carolina _ The Pinkerton Matchmakers
An Agent for Cari - The Pinkerton Matchmakers
A Tin Star for Christmas - The Belles of Wyoming
Stealing Her Heart - The Belles of Wyoming
Candy Cane Christmas - Ornamental Matchmaker Book #10

To see any of the above titles and more new releases stop by Amazon Author Page[1] (http://amzn.to/1PUylgW).

---

1. http://amzn.to/1PUylgW

Don't miss out!

Visit the website below and you can sign up to receive emails whenever Cyndi Raye publishes a new book. There's no charge and no obligation.

https://books2read.com/r/B-A-PXQ-WHMFC

Connecting independent readers to independent writers.

www.ingramcontent.com/pod-product-compliance
Lightning Source LLC
Chambersburg PA
CBHW031424130726
47989CB00003B/1029